Rebekah – Girl Detective

Books 1 - 8

PJ Ryan

Contents

"Rebekah - Girl Detective" is a short story series for children ages 9-12 with the remaining titles to be published on a regular basis. Each title can be read on its own.

You can join Rebekah's fun Facebook page for young detectives here:

http://www.facebook.com/RebekahGirlDetective

I'd really love to hear from you!

I very much appreciate your reviews and comments so thank you in advance for taking a moment to leave one here for "Rebekah - Girl Detective: Books 1-8".

Sincerely,
PJ

All Titles by PJ Ryan Can be Found Here (Author Page)
http://www.amazon.com/author/pjryan

Look for the following series with more coming soon!

Rebekah – Girl Detective
RJ – Boy Detective
Mouse's Secret Club

Rebekah - Girl Detective #1
The Mysterious Garden

Chapter 1

"Chirp, chirp," said the stuffed bear. Rebekah knocked it sideways and glared at the floor behind it.

"Oh I'll find you, beast," she hissed and waved the beam of her flashlight in rapid circles. She had been hunting the cricket for over an hour. It really was not fair to lay down for a nice sleep, only to be awakened by that incessant chirping.

"Chirp, chirp," the bookshelf across the room called out.

"Argh!" Rebekah squealed and lunged in its direction.

"Rebekah!" her mother cried out from the doorway of her attic bedroom. "What in the world are you doing? The whole house can hear you tromping and stomping around up here," she shook her head as she stifled a yawn. "We're trying to sleep."

"Well, so am I," Rebekah frowned. "But there is a cricket in here somewhere, and it will not stop chirping! Shh! Listen," she put her finger to her lips. Her mother stuck her head all the way into the room and listened very closely. After a few moments she sighed.

"Rebekah, I don't hear anything, just go back to bed," she groaned and headed down the stairs. Rebekah lived in a three story house, and her room was the entire third story. It was not as big as it might seem as the roof sloped sharply, but it was her own little world, and she liked it very much. That was, when there was not a cricket living in it with her.

Once her mother was gone, Rebekah collapsed on her bed. She was exhausted from a day of playing soccer and investigating the latest mystery in her tiny town of Curtis Bay. As she stretched out in her small daybed, she tried to fall asleep faster than the cricket could chirp. It always seemed to help her fall asleep to sort through whatever mystery was on her mind.

Rebekah was determined to be the latest and greatest detective to hit the streets and she saw no reason to wait until she was a grown up. At nine, she was certain that she could do a better job than most. So whenever she spotted something even the slightest bit off, she would do her best to get to the bottom of it.

Like, why did the mailman always deliver the mail at the same exact time, except on Thursdays when he delivered a half hour later? Why if garbage cans were put out at the curb standing straight up, were they often found face down when she returned from school?

These were the type of questions that she absolutely had to have answered. Of course it was easy to figure out that Mr. Mason, who was the mailman for her neighborhood was a half hour later on Thursday's because he always stopped by for a free ice cream cone at Lyle's Ice Cream Parlor. The ice cream cones were only free from 3pm to 4pm on Thursdays.

And she soon discovered that it was only polite to place the cans upside down, showing that the trash had been taken and they were empty. But there were also bigger questions to answer, like why did the principal always show up late for school when it rained? Why did recess last five extra minutes on Fridays?

The mystery currently weighing on her mind was the disappearing flowers. Her town had a community garden, and she would always stop by to water the plants. Lately she had noticed that flowers were disappearing! So far she had interviewed the gardener, Mr. Polson.

"And just where are these flowers going?" she had asked, with her notebook flipped open and pen ready to jot down notes.

"I'm not sure," Mr. Polson sighed as he leaned on his shovel.

"Well, they did not just get up and walk away did they?" she asked as politely as she could.

"Well no," Mr. Polson grumbled. "I didn't see any flower footprints."

Rebekah giggled and scribbled that in her notes. "No flower footprints found at the scene."

As she lay in bed, reviewing the clues, she was just about to fall asleep.

"Chirp, chirp!" her pillow cried out.

"Argh!" Rebekah jumped up and threw her pillow across the room. But there was no cricket to be found.

Chapter 2

The next day at school Rebekah was feeling very sleepy. She and the cricket had fought all night. She still had not found that bug.

"Are you okay?" her best friend Mouse asked. Mouse was not called Mouse because of his size, which was average for a boy of nine, but because he always carried around a mouse in his pocket. He reached down and fed the mouse a piece of cheese.

"Which one is that?" Rebekah asked. Mouse had at least twenty mice for pets. He could tell them all apart, but no one else could.

"Einstein," he replied with a grin. "He likes the sunshine."

It was a very bright and sunny day. Normally Rebekah would be looking forward to soccer practice in the afternoon, but today she was dreaming of a nap.

"Anything new on the flower thief?" Mouse asked, and Einstein squeaked for another piece of cheese.

"No," Rebekah sighed and narrowed her eyes as she looked across the playground. "Why would anyone steal flowers, when they could just pick them?" she wondered.

"Maybe they don't like flowers," Mouse suggested with a shrug.

"Who wouldn't like flowers?" Rebekah laughed.

AAACHOO!

They both jumped at the sound of the huge sneeze behind them.

"Oh how I hate spring," Mrs. McGonal moaned as she trudged past them.

"You hate spring?" Rebekah asked quickly. "Why?"

Mrs. McGonal blew her nose in a tissue and then smiled. "Oh sorry, I shouldn't say hate; I just have such terrible allergies to all of the pollen. It is a beautiful time of year for most people, but for me," she held up the box of tissues she was carrying. "It is allergy season."

"Hm," Rebekah whipped out her small notebook and jotted down a note.

"Do you think Mrs. McGonal stole the flowers?" Mouse whispered.

"No," Rebekah frowned. "She may be grumpy, but she is not usually mean. I don't think she would do it."

"Then who?" Mouse asked as he too looked over the playground.

Rebekah scowled across the basketball court at a young boy who was huddled near the water fountain.

"Ernie," she replied with a growl. "I think Ernie is behind this."

"Ernie?" Mouse asked with surprise. "But he's so quiet, and he never bothers anyone."

Ernie was very shy and tended to stay by himself. Whenever they were on the playground he would stay near the water fountain and pretend to be thirsty if anyone walked up to him.

"Exactly," Rebekah nodded firmly. "It is the quiet ones that you have to watch out for. They are always up to something."

Mouse tilted his head to the side, wondering how Ernie could ever be up to anything, but he knew better than to argue with Rebekah. Once she had a suspect, she would not give up until she had proof.

"First, we have to find some evidence," Rebekah smirked as she stood up from the bench she was sitting on.

"And how are you going to do that?" Mouse asked and tucked Einstein back into his pocket as a teacher walked past.

"I'm going to make friends," Rebekah said with a bright smile and began to stride across the playground.

Chapter 3

When Ernie saw Rebekah walking toward him, he ducked his head and pretended to be drinking from the water fountain. Rebekah waited patiently for him to finish. After drinking what must have been a gallon, Ernie looked up at her shyly.

"Thirsty?" she asked and smiled.

"Uh, a little," he nodded.

"I'm Rebekah," she held out her hand in a friendly way of saying hello.

"I know," he cleared his throat and stared at her hand.

"Just a little handshake," she widened her smile and wiggled her fingers.

Ernie blushed and wiped his hand on his jeans before he shook hers. She grabbed his hand tightly and flipped it over, studying his nails closely.

"Hm, Ernie, I see there is soil under your fingernails," she leaned a little closer.

"Hey," Ernie protested and tugged his hand free. "What's this about?" he demanded and shoved his hands into his pockets.

Rebekah began to march solemnly back and forth with her hands clasped behind her back. "This is about flowers Ernie," she glanced over at him sharply. "Stolen flowers, from the community garden."

Ernie winced and shuffled his feet. "I don't know anything about that," he muttered.

"So you've never been to the garden?" Rebekah suddenly asked.

"Well, I didn't say that," he mumbled and cringed.

"Which is it Ernie, you know nothing, or you know something?" Rebekah demanded, poking her nose close to his.

"Neither, both, ugh!" Ernie covered his face with his hands. He was trembling like a leaf. Rebekah would have felt badly, were it not for the tell tale soil under his fingernails.

"Well, well, Ernie. I think I have caught my flower thief," she smirked.

"No you haven't," he growled and shook his head. "I go to the garden at night, because I am too shy to volunteer," he held out his fingernails. "They get dirty because I weed the garden."

Rebekah's eyebrow shot high up along her forehead. "And I am supposed to believe you because?"

Ernie hung his head. "I don't know, but it's true. You can ask Mr. Polson he is the one that lets me in."

Rebekah tapped her chin thoughtfully. She whipped out her small notepad and scribbled down this new information.

Mr. Polson has secrets!! She wrote.

"You're off the hook," Rebekah said and started to walk away, then she stopped, and turned back. "For now," she added in a gravelly voice.

Ernie gulped, and went for another drink of water.

Chapter 4

Later that day when Rebekah arrived at the community garden she decided to check out Ernie's story.

"Mr. Polson, does a kid named Ernie come here at night to weed the garden?" she asked before even saying hello.

"Why yes," Mr. Polson nodded. "Ernie's a good kid. He always cleans up the garden nicely, and makes sure things are tidied up before he leaves."

"And you don't think he has anything to do with the disappearing flowers?" Rebekah asked as she whipped out her notepad and poised her pen above it.

"No way," Mr. Polson shook his head. "Ernie wouldn't do anything to hurt the flowers."

Rebekah sighed as she realized that so far she had two suspects, but neither of them seemed to be the culprit. She wondered if that cricket keeping her awake at night was causing her to lose her detective mojo. She decided to spend some time watering the flowers, so that she could think things through. Her favorite watering can was lime green and had a deep bucket. It could water nearly the entire garden without having to be refilled, but it was a bit heavy. The garden was filled with all different colors and types of flowers. It even had a section for berries and vegetables. Anyone in the community could donate a small fee, and take from the garden a portion of the food. It was a great resource for the entire neighborhood. That was why it seemed so odd to her that anyone would want to hurt or destroy it. As she reached the end of the garden, she gasped.

"Mr. Polson!" she shouted in a high pitched voice.

"What is it? Are you okay?" he asked as he ran up out of breath.

13

"Look!" Rebekah pointed to the empty holes where flowers had once been. "How could more be gone?" she moaned.

"Well I just don't know," Mr. Polson sighed and scratched his head. "It's a real mystery."

"Yes, yes it is," Rebekah said with a frown. She finished watering the flowers and then hurried off to soccer practice.

Mouse sat on the bleachers watching Rebekah played. He preferred to watch sports, rather than play them. Rebekah chased the ball up and down the field. She always played better when she had a mystery on her mind. By the time practice was over, the coach was praising her for her speed.

"Great job Rebekah, you really hustled out there."

Rebekah took a big gulp of her water and smiled. "Thanks coach," she said, but her smile soon faded. She could not get the missing flowers off of her mind.

"I think tonight, we should check on our friend Ernie ourselves," she said to mouse as she took another drink.

"I don't know Rebekah, he seems so shy, we might upset him," Mouse warned.

"Or we might catch him stealing flowers," she replied darkly.

"Alright," Mouse nodded, but he was not convinced.

Chapter 5

They waited until sunset and then returned to the community garden. Mr. Polson was just leaving, and they could see Ernie in the garden, weeding by the overhead lights. There was no one else in the garden with him.

"Let's go," Rebekah said from behind the parked car they had hidden behind.

"Rebekah, are you sure?" Mouse started to ask, but it was too late. Rebekah was already walking into the garden.

"Hello there Ernie," she said as she crossed her arms and settled her eyes on him. Ernie jumped right out of his skin, at least that's what it felt like. He looked up at Rebekah and winced.

"What is it now?" he asked with a frown. "See, just weeds," he held up the weeds in his hands.

"Likely story," Rebekah mumbled and began to pace back and forth behind him.

"Oh Rebekah it looks like he's just weeding the garden," Mouse hissed when he caught up with her.

"Yes, that's what it looks like," she said quietly.

All of the sudden the lights above them began flickering like strobe light.

"What's happening?" Mouse asked nervously as he looked up at the lights. Rebekah was puzzled as she watched the lights flicker.

"Very suspicious," she mumbled as she looked around the garden.

"It's been happening the past couple nights," Ernie admitted. "I told Mr. Polson, but he didn't find anything wrong with the lights," he lowered his voice. "It's really kind of spooky."

15

Rebekah started to walk toward one of the lights, but as she did, all of the lights suddenly went completely dark. The sun had finished setting, and the garden was very dark since there were no houses or buildings too close to it.

"Ah!" Mouse gasped. "What could make the lights go out?"

"Maybe our flower thief is more clever than we thought," Rebekah frowned.

"Maybe it's a ghost," Ernie suggested. "Ghosts like the dark."

"He's right, it could be a ghost," Mouse said quickly.

"No it couldn't," Rebekah countered. "Even if ghosts were real, which they are not, why would a ghost be in a garden? Why would a ghost steal flowers?"

Ernie lifted his chin high in the air. "You're the investigator, aren't you?"

Rebekah rolled her eyes and pulled out her keys from her pocket. She had a small penlight attached to her key chain so that she would always be able to see into small dark spaces. It didn't do much to light up the garden, but at least she could see if anymore flowers were disappearing. When she saw the leaves of one plant rustling she rushed forward, expecting to catch the thief. Instead her foot found an empty space where ground should have been.

"Ugh," she gasped as she lost her balance and her ankle twisted. She had stepped into a hole in the ground. She fell forward and managed to break her fall with her hands. She flopped on the ground and blew her hair out of her face as she looked up at the two boys above her.

"Are you okay?" they asked at the same time.

"I think so," she replied, and looked past them at the plant that had been shaking. Only, there was no plant to see. It had disappeared!

"Oh, the thief got another one!" she sighed and sat up in the dirt. Her shoulders slumped.

"Some investigator I am," she shook her head.

"You're a great investigator," Mouse said firmly.

"Yeah, you sure try hard," Ernie encouraged. "Look how close you came."

"Yes that's true," Rebekah nodded. "I would have caught that thief if it weren't for the trap it set for me," she growled and glared at the hole she had tripped in. "Who would go around a garden digging holes?"

"Uh, a gardener?" Mouse muttered.

"Maybe a gh-"

"Don't say ghost," Rebekah growled. She tapped her chin lightly as she thought about the situation. Somehow the thief had managed to turn out all of the lights in the garden. The thief had also left behind traps to keep her from catching it.

"This is a very stealth thief," she said quietly. She crept over to the hole she had tripped in. It was just big enough for her foot to get stuck in. She shone the penlight into the hole.

"Wow," she gasped as she gestured to Mouse and Ernie to look closer. "It's not a hole at all."

"It's a tunnel!" Mouse cried out.

"Creepy," Ernie shuddered. "Maybe it is gigantic underground worm," he cringed.

Rebekah tucked her penlight between her teeth and pulled out her notebook from her pocket. She opened it up and made a few notes on the paper.

"Oh it's an underground something," she mumbled and glanced up at the darkened lights.

17

Chapter 6

Rebekah was very tired when she laid down that night. She had showered all of the dirt from the garden off of her and put a little ice on her sore ankle. She hoped it would not keep her from playing well in the soccer game on Saturday. As she sat on her bed she picked up the tablet she had borrowed from her father. With it she could access information about all kinds of creatures. She began using the information she had collected to look up what might be hiding underground in the garden. It had to be a very stealth animal, it had to be capable of knocking out electricity, and snatching whole flowers. As she put the information into the tablet she was disappointed that she did not get any results. In a moment of desperation, she typed in, gigantic underground worm.

"Ugh!" she shrieked when the image of a huge worm burst on to the screen. "Bleh," she shivered and turned the tablet off. She would just have to take another look at the garden in the light of day. As she was just about to fall asleep, she heard the sound.

"Chirp, chirp," said her windowsill.

"Oh no," she moaned and buried her head under her pillow. If it wasn't one mysterious creature, it was another.

She woke early the next morning and hurried to get ready for school. Her mother had toast and eggs waiting for her, but she buzzed right past.

"Sorry Mom, too busy, I'm on a case," she called out and was just about out the front door when her mother hooked the strap on her book bag and tugged her backwards.

"Even detectives need breakfast Rebekah," she said firmly and dropped a piece of toast into her daughter's hand.

"Thanks mom," Rebekah grinned and kissed her cheek lightly. Then she ran out the front door. She ran all the way to the community garden, taking bites of toast along the way.

Chapter 7

When she reached the garden Mr. Polson was already there. He was digging a few fresh holes to plant some fruit trees in, and didn't hear Rebekah when she came running up behind him.

"We have a big problem!" she announced in a shrill voice. Mr. Polson nearly dropped his shovel. He sighed and wiped at his brow as he turned to look at Rebekah.

"What is it now Rebekah?" he asked impatiently.

"Have you tried the lights yet this morning?" she asked and pointed to the lights that surrounded the garden.

"Well no," he said with a frown. "They're on a timer, and they don't come on in the daylight."

"Well, they won't work," she said firmly.

"Why? What happened here last night?" he demanded with concern. "I can't let you kids be in the garden after hours if you're going to break things."

"It wasn't us," Rebekah protested as Mr. Polson tried to switch the lights on.

"Oh no," he frowned. "Now what are we going to do with no lights? Something most have cut off the electricity," he sighed and began looking over the garden for any sign of what could cause the problem. Rebekah followed along behind him.

"I also found tunnels in the ground," she said quickly and pointed out the hole she had tripped on the night before.

"Oh did you," he said quietly and crouched down to peer into the hole. "Well now things are starting to make sense," he smiled a little.

"You mean gigantic underground worms?" Rebekah suggested.

"Oh no," he laughed. "Much worse. Cuter, and furrier, but much worse."

Rebekah was confused, until Mr. Polson leaned closer to her and whispered something her ear.

"Oh!" Rebekah cried out with surprise.

"Look you're going to be late for school," Mr. Polson said as he glanced at his watch. "I'll do a little more research, and after school, meet me here, okay?" he asked.

Rebekah nodded with a frown. She hated to head to school right in the middle of a mystery, but she didn't like to miss her classes either. As she walked the rest of the way to school her mind was filled with all kinds of ideas, of how to trap the flower thief. She just hoped that one of them would work.

Chapter 8

At school, Mouse ran up to her with a wide grin. "Guess what, I looked up all of this information about gigantic underground worms last night," he gushed.

"Ugh Mouse it is not a gigantic underground worm," Rebekah insisted.

"Oh I know, but still, these worms are fascinating!" he continued to grin.

"That's one way to describe them," she said reluctantly. As they were walking to class, Ernie stood shyly by his locker. When he saw them coming he looked up nervously.

"Hi Ernie," Rebekah said in a friendly tone.

Ernie smiled a little. "Hi guys," his smile brightened when they stopped to talk with him.

"Did you figure out what made those tunnels?" he asked hopefully. He loved going to the garden, and didn't want to be too scared to go back.

"Mr. Polson has an idea," Rebekah said with a smile. "And I think he may be right. But we will have to see if we can catch the thief. Do you want to help?"

Ernie was surprised to be invited. He was sure that he was still Rebekah's suspect. Besides, he never got invited to anything. It made him feel great that Rebekah and Mouse seemed to want him to be there.

"Well, I guess," he said shyly. "I mean, if you want me to."

"Of course we do," Mouse said. "I mean, who else is going to protect us from the gigantic underground worm," he held up a picture he had printed off of his computer. "See?"

"Ah!" Ernie jumped back against his locker, and then all three of the friends began to laugh. Just then the bell that signaled the start of their first class rang. They scattered to their classes, not wanting to be late. At recess, Mouse, Ernie, and Rebekah huddled around her notebook. She was going over the clues she had gathered during her investigation. With each one she felt it was more likely that the creature that Mr. Polson suspected was the flower thief.

"How could something so small do so much damage?" Mouse wondered.

Einstein poked his head up out of his pocket. "No not you Einstein," Mouse laughed and patted the tiny creatures head. Ernie offered him a piece of cheese form his sandwich. Einstein nibbled it gone in no more than a second.

"Cute," he laughed.

"He's got tons," Rebekah sighed.

"Not tons," Mouse corrected. "Just, plenty," he smiled broadly.

As they left school that day they promised to meet up after dark at the community garden. Instead of heading home though, Rebekah went straight to the garden. Mr. Polson was waiting there for her with an extra shovel.

"Here you go," he said as he handed her one of the shovels. "Let's get to work."

They found each and every hole that had been made in the garden. Carefully they filled the tunnels with dirt, until only one remained.

"Looks like our little thief chewed through the electrical wires," he sighed and shook his head. "They are hard creatures to nab, are you sure that you're up for this Rebekah?"

"Absolutely," she replied. "No more flowers will go missing on my watch," she said firmly. Mr. Polson handed her a cage he had bought that day and explained to her how to set the trap.

Chapter 9

Rebekah, Mouse, and Ernie gathered at the garden just after dark. They were armed with flashlights and ready to catch a flower thief. She and Mr. Polson had filled in every hole in the garden, except for one. Near that one, the three set up a trap, a cage with a tasty plant waiting inside, for the flower thief. If it was hungry, it would be forced to come out of that one hole, and find the plant waiting for it.

The trap was set, and Rebekah was excited to see if her and Mr. Polson's theory was right. She, Mouse, and Ernie all huddled down behind a large wheelbarrow, waiting to see if their flower napper would dare to appear. The bright light of the moon was enough to illuminate the garden, and shine on every single petal. It was a perfect night for capturing a flower thief.

"What if we're wrong," whispered Mouse. "What if we sit out here all night, and nothing happens?" he frowned as he swatted at an insect that was flying around him.

"We're not wrong," Rebekah insisted. She pulled her notebook out of her pocket and reviewed the clues that she had picked up along the way.

"It is a stealth thief; it comes and goes without anyone seeing. It leaves no footprints behind. It takes the whole plant, roots and all."

"But what if it isn't what we think at all," Ernie wondered through chattering teeth. "What if it's some kind of magical elf that is collecting flowers from our world? Maybe, once it has enough flowers, it will want to collect children!"

Mouse and Rebekah both looked at Ernie with wide disbelieving eyes. "Are you serious?" Rebekah asked and quirked a brow.

"It could happen," Ernie said with a frown. "I've seen it on television."

"Ernie," Mouse said patiently. "Don't you think if the magical elf wanted children, it would be at the school, not in the community garden?"

Ernie sighed. "I guess you're right," he fell silent.

"Or, it could be that magical elves don't exist," Rebekah pointed out and shook her head at the two boys.

"You don't know," they both said sharply.

"Actually, I do," Rebekah said sternly. "I have investigated many magical creatures, and none of them have any basis in science."

"Hm, that's why they're called magical," Ernie rolled his eyes and Mouse snickered.

"Argh,' Rebekah sighed and looked back at the trap they had set." Shh, we might scare it off if we talk too loud."

"Squeak, squeak, squeak!" a loud noise began filling the air around them.

"Ernie, please stop squeaking," Rebekah said as patiently as she could.

"It's not me," Ernie squeaked, then cleared his throat. "I mean, it's not me," he said sternly.

They both looked at Mouse who had his hand over his pocket. "Einstein, shh," he said and tried to quite the mouse in his pocket.

"What has him so upset? Out of cheese?" Rebekah asked.

"No, I don't know what's wrong," Mouse frowned. "He is never this noisy."

"Maybe he knows the magical elf is coming," Ernie whispered, his voice shaking.

"Ernie," Rebekah growled.

Just then Einstein managed to wriggle his way out of Mouse's pocket, and went racing across the garden in a swift white streak.

"Einstein!" Mouse cried out and started chasing after him.

"Shh!" Rebekah hissed. While they were looking at the fleeing rodent nobody noticed the pair of eyes that were peeking up out of the ground right beside the trap they had set.

Ernie was the first to notice the beady stare. "Th-that's not an elf," he gasped and started stumbling backwards. When he did, he knocked over the large watering can, and water began spilling everywhere. Mouse was still chasing after Einstein and Rebekah turned back in time to see what Ernie was pointing at.

"Oh! It's you!" she growled and crouched down. "Come on little flower thief, take the bait!"

As she and Ernie huddled close together they watched the small animal crawl out of the only hole they had left unfilled. It crept slowly across the soil toward the beautiful plant they had left in prime view, just waiting to be stolen.

Just as the gopher was about to scuttle right into the trap, Einstein went running past, followed closely by Mouse. The gopher squealed and ran for his hole.

"Oh no he's getting away!" Ernie cried out and started to run for the gopher, but he slipped in the mud that had been created by the spilled watering can, and landed on his back. "Owwww," he complained. Rebekah lunged after the gopher and just before it could escape back into its tunnel she managed to flip the wheelbarrow over on top of the small opening, blocking the gopher's way.

"No escaping justice!" she declared and glowered at the gopher. The gopher of course was not in the mood to be caught, so he began digging furiously in the ground to make a new tunnel.

Before he could though, Mouse with Einstein finally tucked back into his pocket, managed to lift the small cage they had prepared to catch the gopher, and scoop the creature up with it. Once the cage was locked all three gathered close to peer between the narrow bars.

"He doesn't look so bad," Mouse cooed, and Einstein poked his head out to say hello.

"He's actually kind of cute," Ernie admitted and clucked his tongue at the gopher.

"Cute?" Rebekah narrowed his eyes. "Oh no my friends, this gopher has been living a life of crime. He has been stealing our flowers right out from under our noses, and there is nothing cute about that. Bad gopher!" she wagged her finger at the gopher. It sniffed at her finger and grunted.

"See, he's confessing," Rebekah said confidently.

"Aw come on Rebekah, he's really just like a big mouse-" Mouse started to say.

"No Mouse, your mother is not going to let you keep a gopher as a pet."

"Maybe she would," Mouse protested.

"Nope, no way," Rebekah shook her head. "Your mother will not have a thief living under her roof."

Mouse sighed.

Ernie frowned.

Rebekah whipped out her notepad and jotted down a note to declare the crime of the stolen flowers officially solved.

Chapter 10

The next morning Mr. Polson arrived at the community garden to find the gopher still sitting in its cage.

"Well hello there little fellow," he chuckled. "Looks like Rebekah caught her thief after all."

He picked up the cage and carried it to his truck. He drove to an open area with plenty of lush wild plants and flowers for the gopher to devour.

As Rebekah settled in for bed that night she sighed with relief. For now the community garden was safe and free of pests, now if only she could say the same about her bedroom.

"Chirp, chirp," said her bookshelf.

"Chirp, chirp," said her windowsill.

"Chirp, chirp," said her teddy bear.

"Oh no," Rebekah groaned and buried her head under her pillow.

Rebekah - Girl Detective #2
Alien Invasion

Chapter 1

"Rebekah how does it feel to be the first ten year old to go into space?" the reporter asked and then shoved the microphone into Rebekah's face. Rebekah, dressed in a lime green space suit, with her bright red curls tucked into her very own space helmet smiled.

"It is a great honor," she said. She looked over at the space ship. It was shaped like a circle. Around its curve Rebekah was printed out in bold white letters.

"What will be your first stop Rebekah?" the reporter asked. "The moon? Mars?"

"I am planning on getting to the bottom of Saturn's rings," she replied and lifted her eyes to the crowd around her. "There is something very strange about those rings. I think that planet may be hiding something."

"Rebekah," the reporter called out. "Rebekah!" she said in a more upset tone.

"I said, Saturn," Rebekah frowned.

"Rebekah!" her mother's voice shouted.

Rebekah's eyes snapped open and she rolled over in her bed. She was not in a lime green space suit. There was no reporter in her room. It had all been just a dream. But she still wondered about that sneaky Saturn.

"I'm up, I'm up," Rebekah called out sleepily. Rebekah was normally the first person awake in her family. She liked to keep an eye on everyone and everything and sleep got in the way of that. But the night before she and her best friend Mouse had been out in the backyard very late studying the stars with her brand new telescope. Of course this had stirred up all kinds of questions for her. Science was still one of the great mysteries in her mind. Sure a lot of things had been discovered, but there was still so much more to learn about and get to the bottom of.

Chapter 2

When she reached science class she was excited to see that Mr. Woods had set up a projector in the class. She liked it when he showed slides of different bacteria and organisms. Today, however, that was not what he was showing slides of.

"Today we are going to talk about life on other planets," Mr. Woods said as he dimmed the lights in the classroom. Rebekah looked over at Mouse who was busy trying to make sure his friend for the day, Whiskers, was still safely tucked into his pocket. He knew one incident of one of his mouse friends escaping would get him into some very big trouble.

Rebekah huffed and raised her hand, demanding Mr. Woods' attention.

"Yes Rebekah?" he asked as he situated the projector so that its images would shine on the white screen he had pulled down in front of the chalkboard.

"Mr. Woods, you can't seriously be teaching a class on aliens," Rebekah said with her chin raised high in the air.

Mr. Woods smiled patiently as he looked at Rebekah. He was a fun teacher most of the time. His hair was always wild and sticking up in different directions. He wore slightly bent glasses that were always crooked on his nose, making his blue eyes look like they were two different sizes. His clothes were always rumpled, and at least three days out of the week he found a reason to wear a white lab coat. He was surely one of Rebekah's more liked teachers, but she did not expect such a silly class from a science teacher.

"Yes, I am teaching a class about the possibility of life on other planets," he said with a smile. "Who is to say what is beyond what we know?"

"Uh, I believe that science has made it clear there is no life on other planets," Rebekah pointed out.

"Actually, one of the girls sitting in the front of the class spoke up." The Mars Rover recently discovered that water was once on the planet and that it might have been habitable. Maybe they will find out that there was once life on it!" she said, her voice full of excitement.

"There is a big difference between aliens and microbes," Rebekah said sternly. The girl in the front of the class was Libby, and she was rather strange in Rebekah's opinion. She was always wearing t-shirts that had funny pictures of aliens and strange animals on them.

"Maybe Rebekah," Mr. Woods agreed. "And I am not here to tell you that there is life on other planets, I am just curious what you might think life would be like on other planets."

"It wouldn't exist," Rebekah said sternly.

"I think it would be much better than ours," Libby spoke up. "I bet aliens are much more peaceful than we are."

"No, aliens are not real," Rebekah said firmly.

"Rebekah, everyone is allowed to have their own ideas," Mr. Woods warned. "We should let Libby share hers too."

Libby looked over her shoulder at Rebekah and smiled.

Rebekah forced a smile back and then slumped down in her chair. She did not like where this class was going. For the rest of the class Mr. Woods showed slides of different images of aliens that people had reported seeing or imagined that aliens would look like. At the end of the class he gave an assignment.

"I want each of you to take some time tonight and think about what a being from another planet might look like. Then you can draw this image for me, and tomorrow we can take a look at everyone's ideas. I think you might be surprised by how different they will be."

Rebekah rolled her eyes and muttered under her breath about how pointless the assignment was. It was not that she didn't like drawing, but she felt talking about aliens in science class was silly. As the kids started to leave the classroom she fell into step beside Mouse.

"This is crazy isn't it?" she asked him.

"What is?" he tucked his hand in his pocket to keep Whiskers calm.

"Drawing pictures of aliens. Who really believes in aliens?" she asked.

"I do," Libby said from behind them.

"Well you're wrong," Rebekah said as she turned around to face Libby.

"How do you know?" Libby asked with a smile. She was a friendly girl, just not very bright, in Rebekah's opinion.

"Because, it has been proven again and again," Rebekah said and shook her head.

"Not all things can be proven or ruled out by science, at least not yet Rebekah, you should be a little more open about it," Libby suggested sweetly. Then she looked at Mouse.

"How's Whiskers?" she asked and peeked in his pocket when he held it open for her to see.

"Happy," he smiled. "She likes the cheese you told me about," he said. When Libby walked away, Rebekah looked at him curiously.

"What cheese?"

"Oh I was having a hard time getting him to stay in my pocket, so Libby gave me some goat cheese to try," he smiled and held out a crumble of the cheese.

"Ew," Rebekah scrunched up her nose. "That is smelly!"

"Yeah it is, but Whiskers likes it!" he smiled.

"Well she may know her cheese, but she sure doesn't know her science," Rebekah smirked.

"Are you sure?"

Mouse asked and twitched his nose, not unlike his pet mouse did.

"Of course I am sure," Rebekah sighed. "Don't tell me you believe all of this stuff too!"

"I don't believe it," he said with a shrug. "I just don't not believe it either. I mean, lots of things are possible today that we didn't think were possible in the past, so maybe just maybe, we don't know everything," he offered her a silly grin.

"Maybe," Rebekah said thoughtfully. She had never even considered that aliens could be real. But now that she thought about it, she was curious.

That afternoon when she got home from school she sat down in front of her computer. She knew that if there were aliens, someone must have seen them. There had to be some proof somewhere. She started looking up information on aliens. The more she looked up, the more shocked she became. There was a lot of information about aliens and people who said they had seen them. One site, the scariest of all, said that some aliens could even look like and talk like human beings!

"How will we ever know who is an alien if they look like us?" Rebekah wondered with horror. She printed off a list of things to look for when looking for an alien.

1. Flashing or floating lights in the sky. These floating lights could be alien space craft looking for a good place to land, or other aliens that have already landed!

2. Odd behavior or a strange appearance. If someone you meet seems very weird, you might just have met an alien.

3. Oddly shaped eyes. Aliens have huge eyes that are hard to hide. If you see someone with eyes that are strange colors or shapes, this might be an alien.

4. Glowing or green skin. If someone seems to be glowing, or has green patches on their skin, this might be their true alien being shining through their human disguise.

She still was not sure if she believed in aliens, but it was good to have a list to use to spot them, just in case. She tucked the list into her camera case and then continued to search. She was a little surprised to find that while there was no scientific proof of aliens, people had been spotting aliens for many years. Some people even thought aliens lived right along beside them. It was an odd idea, and one that Rebekah was sure was not true, but still, she did have to wonder.

Chapter 3

That night at dinner she settled her gaze on her mother and father.

"Are there aliens?" she asked and took a bite of her macaroni and cheese.

"Uh, well, some people believe there are," her father said, his red mustache hiding his frown.

"But many people believe there aren't," her mother said as she smiled.

"That's not an answer," Rebekah sighed and pushed her broccoli around her plate.

"Well sweetie, not everything in the world has an answer," her father said quietly.

"But there must be an answer," Rebekah insisted. "It's just like school when you take a test. You might not always know the right answer, but there is always an answer."

Her mother pointed to her broccoli. "Now you eat that up or you're not getting desert," she warned, before continuing. "It is true that we know a lot about the world around us sweetie, but there are some things we don't even know how to ask questions about. If you don't know every little thing about the universe, well then, you just can't be sure that you have all the answers."

Rebekah was disappointed that her parents could not give her a straight answer. She usually relied on them to help her figure things out that she wasn't sure about. She polished off her broccoli while still thinking about the aliens.

"Well there's one thing I can be sure of," she said glumly as she chewed her last bite of broccoli. "If there are aliens, I bet they don't make their kids eat broccoli."

"Rebekah," her father warned.

"Rebekah!" her mother sighed.

"I know, I know, just eat it," she pouted. When she finished dinner she helped her mother clear the plates. After they shared some ice cream she decided that she would just have to look into this matter herself. She waited until it was very dark, then she grabbed her jacket. She went out back and set up her telescope. Mouse couldn't come over because it was a school night, so she called him on her phone instead.

"Hi, what are you doing?" he asked around a mouthful of popcorn.

"I'm hunting aliens, what are you doing?" she asked with a grin.

He coughed on his popcorn. "You're doing what?" he gasped.

"I'm using my telescope to see if I can find any aliens," she explained and then took a peek through the telescope. "So far, I see stars and more stars."

"Wow, Libby really made you think, hm?" he asked.

"Well I looked it up, and it seems that Libby might be on to something, might," she repeated.

"You never know," he agreed. Rebekah was just about to say goodbye when she saw something strange in the sky.

"What is that?" she wondered as she peered through the telescope.

"Do you see something?" Mouse asked hopefully.

"I think I do," she replied, a little frightened. There was a bright light moving around in the sky. It was much too close to be a star and much too high to be the headlights from a car.

"What is it?" Mouse asked.

46

"I don't know," she whispered and adjusted the telescope. The light was moving this way and that. It even flashed once or twice.

"Oh no," she groaned as she realized what direction it was coming from.

"What's wrong?" Mouse asked, eager to know what was happening.

"It's a strange light, and it looks like it is coming from the school!" she cried out. She remembered the first thing on her list of things to watch for, it was strange lights.

"The school?" Mouse repeated and laughed. "You're just trying to scare me."

"No I'm not," Rebekah insisted. "I think there is something very strange going on here."

"You always think something strange is going on," he reminded her, but his voice was shaky.

"But think about it Mouse, what if there really are aliens in our school?" she asked with fear in her voice.

"That's not possible," Mouse said firmly.

"Like Libby would say, anything is possible," Rebekah argued. "All I know for sure is, there is a bright light moving around in the sky and it is right over our school! Maybe they are dropping off aliens, or picking them up!" she shivered at the very idea of sharing her school with real live aliens.

"I don't know Rebekah," Mouse said in a quiet tone. "Why would aliens come to our school?"

"Maybe they're here for Libby," Rebekah shrieked. "That must be it! She called them here, and now they're going to take all of us!"

"Rebekah," her father called from the back door. "It's time for bed."

Rebekah fell backwards dramatically in the grass. "He really thinks I can sleep after all of this?" she wondered out loud.

"I'll see you in the morning Rebekah," Mouse giggled and hung up the phone. Rebekah glared at the phone for a moment. Then she lifted one eyebrow. What kind of kid carried mice around in their pockets anyway? What if it wasn't Libby at all that the aliens were after? Maybe it was Mouse!

Chapter 4

The next day when Rebekah arrived at school she was ready to see if there were any aliens hanging around. She waited out front for Mouse to arrive. When he did he looked a little worried.

"What's wrong?" Rebekah asked and watched him closely.

"Oh, just had a little accident," he sighed and covered up the pocket in his shirt.

"What kind of accident?" Rebekah asked feeling a little more suspicious.

"Well, I was making my picture of what I thought alien life might be like. And of course, I thought it would be really interesting if there were aliens that looked like mice," he sighed heavily. "But everyone knows aliens are green, so I was using green paint and-"

Whiskers poked his head up out of Mouse's shirt pocket. He was completely green! Rebekah gasped. She looked from the green mouse to her friend Mouse and narrowed her eyes. He was a very strange person. But that was why she liked him. It did seem odd to her that he was always carrying around mice, but that was just how Mouse was.

"Are you sure it's paint?" Rebekah asked and poked a finger lightly at the mouse. Whiskers squeaked back at her.

"Yes, of course it is," Mouse replied. "Unless you think he was abducted by aliens, and they turned him green!" he laughed loudly. Rebekah did not laugh as she looked at Mouse more closely.

"Hm," she said softly.

"Rebekah!" Mouse glared back. "Whiskers is not an alien mouse!"

"Alright, but what about you?" Rebekah asked and tapped her chin lightly.

"Me?" Mouse threw his hands up in the air. "Of course I am not an alien. Do I look like an alien to you?"

Rebekah looked from Mouse's mad face to the green palms of his hands.

"Uh," she said and pointed at his hands.

Mouse looked at his hands. "Oh Rebekah," he cried out. "It's just paint, see," he pulled out the picture of alien mice he had painted the night before, to show her. There were several green mice on a planet made of bright yellow cheese.

"Wouldn't they eat their own planet?" she asked and scrunched up her nose.

"Oh, I didn't really think about that," he said with a frown. "Where's yours?"

All of the sudden Rebekah remembered that she had homework the night before.

"Oh no, I didn't do it," Rebekah frowned. "I'll get a zero."

Mouse looked up at the clock as they walked into the school. "You still have time," he said.

"But I need to figure out who the alien is," she reminded him.

"So you know it's not me?" he grinned.

"Yes, Mouse, you're too weird to be an alien!" she laughed.

He ducked down into a bow. "Thank you, thank you!"

When they reached science class Rebekah was very worried that she would get in trouble for not having her homework. She sat down at her desk and began scribbling together a design.

"What is that supposed to be?" Libby asked as she peered over Rebekah's shoulder. Rebekah had drawn very tall stick figure aliens. She made their eyes as big as saucers and fished a green colored pencil out of her bag to give them a green glow.

"Aliens," Rebekah shrugged.

"Those are not aliens," Libby giggled. "Aliens are short."

"How do you know?" Rebekah asked and looked up at Libby quickly. Maybe there was a reason she wore all those t-shirts and believed in aliens. Maybe it was because Libby was the alien!

"I've read lots of books," Libby said proudly. "Aliens are short, and some are green, but some are gray. They do have big eyes though."

Rebekah looked Libby over closely for any sign that she might be an alien. She did not have any green glowing skin. Her eyes were small and brown. Other than liking aliens, she really was not very strange.

"Have you ever seen one?" Rebekah asked in a whisper.

"Oh yes all the time!" Libby said happily.

"Really?" Rebekah gasped.

"Well, I mean in movies and on television," Libby said. "I've never seen a real alien in person."

Rebekah sighed with disappointment. She pulled out the list she had printed out.

"Does this make sense to you?" she asked.

Libby read the list over and then nodded. "Yes, I'd say it's a good list."

Mr. Woods walked into the room, and Libby smiled.

"Good luck with your, uh, picture," she said as she hurried off to her desk.

Rebekah looked down at her crude drawing and cringed. She hoped Mr. Woods would not be too upset with her. Before she could look up at him, he suddenly switched off the lights. The room began to glow.

"Oh no!" Rebekah cried out. "The aliens are here!"

Chapter 5

"Rebekah!" Mr. Woods hollered as all of the kids in the class began screaming and hiding. "There are no aliens here," he huffed and flicked on the light. "I was just trying to make it fun for us to show off our pictures. Is everyone okay?" he looked around at the still frightened students. Rebekah was the only one standing on top of her desk with her science book held above her head ready to smash some aliens.

"Get down this instant," Mr. Woods growled.

Rebekah winced and climbed down off of her desk. "Now what in the world made you say something like that?" he asked.

"Well, the room was glowing," Rebekah muttered as a few of the other kids snickered at her.

"Yes, well glow in the dark stars will do that," Mr. Woods said as he pointed to the glow in the dark stars he had hung from the ceiling.

"Oh," Rebekah said quietly. Her cheeks were burning. She was usually so calm and could figure out any mystery, but this one had her on edge.

"Now young lady, since you wanted to cause so much chaos, you can present your picture first," he crossed his arms.

Rebekah picked up her quickly sketched, half-finished picture.

"Oh I see," Mr. Woods said with a shake of his head. "You just didn't do your homework and were hoping that the aliens would save you?"

Rebekah sighed as she looked at her shoes. "Well, I read something about aliens pretending to be people, and I-"

"Rebekah," Mr. Woods looked her straight in the eye. "I will not have you scaring the other kids. There are plenty of ideas about aliens out there, but this class is meant to be for fun. It is not meant to be scary. There are no aliens pretending to be humans."

Rebekah opened her mouth to say something else, but Mr. Woods shook his head.

"Sit down," he pointed to Rebekah's desk. Rebekah sat down. But not before she noticed that when Mr. Woods' sleeve pulled away from his wrist, there was a glimmer of green on his skin. Her eyes widened as she stared at him. Throughout the rest of class she noticed his wild hair, his oddly shaped eyes, and his rumpled clothing. He was a very strange teacher. Strange enough to be an alien?

Chapter 6

"Mouse! Mouse!" Rebekah chased him out of class. He stopped in the hallway and turned to look at her.

"What is it?" he asked with a frown. He had been scared when she said there were aliens. He had also been annoyed that he did not get to show off his alien mouse planet because Mr. Woods decided the class was too scary.

"I think Mr. Woods is the alien," Rebekah said, out of breath from calling his name so many times.

"What?" Mouse groaned and slapped his own forehead with his palm. "Rebekah what has gotten into you? Mr. Woods is not an alien! Libby is not an alien and I am not an alien!"

Rebekah pouted a little. "But how do you know?" she asked, her heart beating fast.

"Like Mr. Woods said, there are no aliens pretending to be humans," Mouse said firmly.

Rebekah bit into her bottom lip and tilted her head to the side. She squinted her eyes and tapped her chin.

"But don't you think that's what an alien pretending to be a science teacher would say?" she asked in a rushed whisper.

"Rebekah, Rebekah," Mouse shook his head.

"What about the light I saw?" she reminded him. "I know the difference between stars and light hovering over the school," she said.

"Well," Mouse frowned, he was not sure what the light had been.

"Just trust me," Rebekah pleaded. "I saw Mr. Wood's wrist, and it was green!"

"Like my hands," Mouse showed her his palms again.

"Yes, but, it was glowing!" she said quickly. "I really saw it this time."

Mouse frowned. Rebekah was one of the smartest people he knew. She could solve just about any mystery. But he had never known her to be so afraid.

"Alright Rebekah," he nodded. "Let's figure this out together. But how?"

Rebekah tugged Mouse around the corner in the hallway before Mr. Woods spotted them. "We'll have to check out what he does after school. I bet if he is an alien there will be plenty of evidence in his classroom."

Mouse was used to getting into investigations with Rebekah, but this one was a little different. She was talking about spying on a teacher.

"Don't worry," Rebekah said when she saw his frown. "When we save everyone from an alien science teacher, they will call us heroes!"

Mouse nodded, and from his pocket Whiskers squeaked.

Chapter 7

After school they camped out behind some cars in the staff parking lot. They knew that most of the teachers stayed after school to work on grading and preparation, and that Mr. Woods would do the same. They passed the time by feeding smelly cheese to Whiskers.

"Why is he so afraid?" Rebekah asked as the little mouse ducked back inside of Mouse's pocket.

"He is the littlest mouse of them all," Mouse explained. "The other mice are always getting to the food first, I think he is just used to getting pushed around."

"Poor Whiskers," Rebekah said and offered him some extra cheese. As the sun began to set many teachers started leaving the school.

"Now we just have to wait for Mr. Woods to leave and get in before the janitor locks the doors," Rebekah said quickly.

"What if we get locked in?" Mouse frowned.

"We'll find a way out," Rebekah said firmly.

"Good because I don't want to spend the whole night stuck inside the school," Mouse warned. "I bet it is spooky after dark."

"Oh Mouse, there is no such thing as spooky," she rolled her eyes at the very idea.

"Uh, really, then what do you call a glowing science teacher?" he asked as he pointed to Mr. Woods. He had taken off his lab coat and was walking toward his car. His arms were glowing green!

"I told you!" Rebekah hissed and had to stop herself from doing a happy dance.

"I can't believe it," Mouse gasped. "Our science teacher really is an alien."

"Shh," Rebekah ducked down further behind the car they were hiding behind. As soon as Mr. Woods sat down in his car, they made a quick run toward the back door of the school. Luckily it was not locked yet. They slipped inside.

The empty halls were actually a little spooky. There was no noise of kids laughing, or teachers yelling. There was an eerie quiet.

"Hurry up," Rebekah said as she headed down the hall. Mouse chased after her. When they reached the wing of the school that had the science classrooms, the hall light had already been switched off. It was dark. Except for the door to Mr. Woods' classroom. It was glowing!

"Ugh," Mouse shuddered. "I don't know if we should go in there."

"We have to be brave," Rebekah insisted. "We have to get some proof that Mr. Woods is an alien or no one will believe us," she said and continued down the hall.

When they reached the classroom, they peaked inside. It was glowing green, and in the middle of the glow, also glowing, was a young girl. They could not see her face at first. Then the girl slowly turned around.

"Libby!" Mouse shrieked.

Rebekah clamped her hand over his mouth. "Shh!" she hissed. They heard footsteps coming down the hall.

"We have to help her," Mouse said. "Mr. Woods must have turned her into an alien!"

"Someone's coming," Rebekah whispered and pulled on Mouse's hand.

"Who is it?" Mouse asked with a frown. Rebekah peered down the hall. Out of the darkness, Mr. Woods was walking toward them.

"Ah!" Rebekah covered her own mouth to keep from screaming.

"Run!" Mouse squeaked and they both began running down the hall.

"Rebekah, get back here!" a voice called out loudly.

But neither of them stopped running. They tried every door until they found an open exit. As they ran out across the football field, the sun had set all the way. The football field was dark. Except for a bright light that seemed to be chasing them!

Chapter 8

"Keep running Mouse!" Rebekah called out, trying to hide from the light. It was swinging back and forth across the field.

"I am, I am!" Mouse called back, and then suddenly he stopped. "Oh no," he grabbed the pocket of his shirt. "Oh no! Whiskers is missing!"

"What?" Rebekah stopped running and spun around. "Where is he?"

"I don't know!" Mouse cried out in a panic. "He isn't in my pocket. He must have fallen out while I was running!"

"Find him, find him," Rebekah said quickly. The back door to the school was opening. She could see Mr. Woods standing in the doorway.

"Rebekah!" He called out again when he spotted her on the football field.

"Hurry Mouse," she pleaded.

"I'm trying," Mouse sniffled. "But he's green, and so is the grass!"

"Come on let's just go," Rebekah said and tried to grab Mouse's hand.

"No Rebekah!" he protested. "I can't, I can't leave him here. Mr. Woods will turn him into a real alien mouse. Just like he turned Libby into an alien girl!"

Mr. Woods was running across the field, and Rebekah was very scared. But she knew that Mouse would not leave without Whiskers, and she was not going to leave Mouse behind.

"Okay let's look," she said quickly. They both dropped down to their hands and knees and began searching the grass for the tiny green mouse.

"Looking for this?" a voice asked from right above them.

Mouse and Rebekah looked up slowly to see a green mouse squeaking and sniffing on the green palm of Mr. Woods' hand.

"Oh no, it's too late!" Mouse cried out dramatically and threw himself on the grass. "Mr. Woods turned him into an alien mouse! Look he's glowing!"

Rebekah was too stunned to even try to run. Mr. Woods' hands were glowing a bright green, which made Whiskers look like he was glowing too.

"Stay back alien!" Rebekah shouted as she jumped to her feet. "You might have gotten Whiskers, but you'll never get Mouse!"

Mr. Woods sighed and shook his head as he looked at Mouse pounding his fists on the ground and Rebekah waving her hands in karate chops in his direction.

"I think you two are a little confused," he said calmly and pet the mouse in his hand. "Maybe we should talk about what you think is going on here?"

"You're an alien pretending to be a science teacher," Rebekah said as if it were pretty clear.

Mr. Woods stared Rebekah straight in the eye and slowly lifted one eyebrow.

"I am not an alien Rebekah," he said sternly.

"But your hands," she pointed to his glowing green hands.

"And the light?" Mouse pointed to the bright light.

"And your arms," Rebekah pointed to his glowing arms.

"And Libby!" Mouse cried out. "Oh poor Libby!"

"I'm not an alien," Mr. Woods folded his arms. "I am a science teacher trying to plan a surprise for his students."

"A surprise?" Rebekah asked.

"Yes," he smiled. "I wanted you all to have a taste of some alien fun. So I decorated the classroom with some glowing paint, but," he showed her his hands again with Whiskers still wriggling in them. "Some got stuck on my hands and arms. I have the spotlight hooked up because I want us to be able to come out here and stargaze, and see if we can spot a space ship. But we need to have some light so that no one trips or gets hurt."

"And Libby?" Rebekah asked nervously.

"Libby has a lot of information about aliens, so she offered to help me with the surprise," he sighed and shook his head. "We had the lights out to make sure the classroom would really glow."

"Oh," Rebekah said quietly. She thought for a moment, and then looked up. "Of course, I knew that all along. It was Mouse that thought you were an alien. I mean, after all, aliens are not real!"

Mouse rolled his eyes as he took Whiskers from Mr. Woods.

"Maybe next time you want to investigate something Rebekah, the first thing you should ask, is Mr. Woods, are you an alien?"

Rebekah giggled. "Okay, I will," she said.

"At least we know the glowing paint works," Mr. Woods said with a grin. "Why don't you two come inside and help Libby and I finish up the surprise, okay?"

Mouse and Rebekah nodded and followed Mr. Woods back toward the school.

"Now Mouse, there is a little matter of a little green pet," Mr. Woods said with a frown.

"Uh, it was just part of the surprise?" Mouse said.

"Oh I see," Mr. Woods laughed and patted him lightly on the back. "We'll make sure he's the star of the show!"

Rebekah – Girl Detective #3

Magellan Goes Missing

PJ Ryan

Rebekah - Girl Detective #3

Magellan Goes Missing

Chapter 1

"Oh yes I see," she muttered in her best detective voice. She leaned her hands on the windowsill and stared out the window. It was an ordinary day in her ordinary neighborhood. She had been staring out of her window for quite some time, just hoping to spot something suspicious. She wanted to have an adventure, but she did not think anyone else did. Everyone seemed to have something to do, or something they were interested in. It was the beginning of summer and she was ready to have some fun. Sadly, she had a bit of a cold and could not go swimming just yet. So she decided to do her other favorite activity, detecting. Her mother called it spying. Her father called it being a little nosy. But she called it paying very close attention. She was paying very close attention to the older couple walking down the street with their tiny dog. She was certain that these people must not be as sweet and nice as they looked. She was just about to launch an investigation when her phone rang. She ran over to the stand beside her bed where she charged it.

"Hello?" she said hoping it would be an adventure calling.

"Oh ---- I am so glad you answered," Mouse gushed into the phone. Mouse was her best friend. He collected little mice as pets, so everyone called him Mouse. Actually, maybe she had been the one to start it, but either way, he was now known as Mouse.

"What's wrong?" she asked.

"It's Magellan," he sighed. "He's gone."

"Is that a mouse?" she asked.

"Yes! My favorite mouse!" he cried out.

"Really?" she frowned.

"Alright, they're all my favorite," he said. "But Magellan is so tiny, I am so scared he's lost or hurt somewhere."

"Have you checked all your pockets?" she asked. Mouse liked to carry his pets around with him in his pockets from time to time.

"Yes, and all the usual hiding spots- under the bed, in the closet, in the hamper-"

"In the hamper?" she gasped.

"Yes," he answered.

"Brave mouse," she giggled.

"Listen!" he said, getting frustrated. "It's not funny, I have to find Magellan!"

"I know you do," she said. "I'm sorry, I shouldn't have teased. This sounds like an investigation," she said firmly. "I'll be over in ten minutes."

"Please hurry," Mouse squeaked.

When she hung up the phone her mind was already spinning with ideas. As she walked out of the house she spotted the older couple with their tiny dog. They smiled nicely at her. She smiled back, but she knew they were up to something.

The walk to Mouse's house was not very far. It was only down the street. As she walked along she heard something moving in the brush beside the sidewalk.

"Who's there?" she demanded as she turned to look inside the brush. There was no person small enough to hide in the bushes. Maybe just maybe it was the couple's dog, come back to spy on her. She peeked through the brush to see what was following after her.

In the middle of the twigs and leaves was a small orange cat. It looked up at her with little blue eyes and seemed very sweet.

"Aww, what a cute kitty," she cooed.

That cute kitty wasn't happy that he had been found. He reached out with his sharp little claws and swiped at the finger that she stretched out to pet him.

"Hey!" she protested. "That's my finger!" she snatched it back before its sharp little nails could slice into her skin.

Chapter 2

The orange cat hissed and growled at her. He stood up on his four legs and raised its back as if it would attack.

"Bad kitty!" she said sharply. "Very bad kitty!"

With a scowl she stalked off the rest of the way to Mouse's house. When she knocked on the door he opened it fast.

"I still can't find him!" he said.

"Oh no," she sighed and shook her head. "I'm sorry that you lost Magellan. I just got attacked by a fierce cat!"

"A fierce cat, like a tiger?" Mouse asked with surprise.

"No silly," she said. "But it could have been, for as loud as it snarled, and how sharp its claws are. It almost got my finger!" she showed him her unmarked finger.

"Oh, bad kitty," he shook his head.

"That's what I said," she grinned. "Now let's take a look at what we can do about this missing mouse!"

"Magellan," he reminded her.

"Yes, Magellan," she said. She whipped out her small notebook. "When was the last time you saw your mouse?" she said.

"This morning, after I let them out into their maze." He replied. "He was in the castle with all of the other mice, but I couldn't find him when it was time to put them back in their cage."

"Is there any way out of the maze?" she asked curiously.

"Here, I'll show you," he said. "I just built a new one yesterday."

Mouse's room was loaded with all kinds of inventions he had created to keep his tiny mice happy. He had mice roller coasters, he had mice bicycles, and even a mouse swing set. He walked her over to his newest creation, a large mouse maze complete with castle turrets and a drawbridge. The mice had to eat the cheese to get the drawbridge to lower.

"This is great!" she said with a smile. "I'd love to run through it."

"You'd have to be a bit smaller," Mouse said thoughtfully. She could tell that he was already inventing some ideas in his head as to how to make a life size maze.

"So all of the mice were in here?" she asked and peered closely. "Oh Mouse one of your mice has a big appetite," she said.

"Huh?" Mouse looked at the corner of the maze that she was pointing at. There was a tiny hole chewed through the cardboard of the box.

"Maybe he thought it was cheese," she said.

"Oh no," he smacked his forehead and groaned. "How could I not see that? He could be anywhere!"

"As long as he didn't get out of the house, we can find him," she assured him, "Let's just take a close look at where he might have gone."

"How can we do that?" Mouse asked. "He's so tiny there's no way to know which way he went."

"By being mice," Rebekah said firmly and dropped down on to all fours beside the mouse maze. She began searching along the baseboards for anywhere that the mouse could have hidden. Mouse dropped down beside her and began searching too.

Chapter 3

What they soon discovered was that Mouse did not clean under his bed or desk very often. They did not find any loose mice.

"Hm," Rebekah frowned as she sat back on her heels. "Maybe we are looking at this the wrong way," she said thoughtfully. "Maybe it isn't that Magellan got out, maybe something else got in."

"What could get in?" Mouse asked.

All of the sudden Rebekah gasped. "I know! That feisty cat I saw in the bushes!"

"How could a cat get in here?" Mouse shook his head with disbelief.

Rebekah pointed to his window. The curtains were blowing in a light breeze. When they walked over to it, they could see the screen was hanging out.

"How did that happen?" Mouse wondered.

"Well, maybe that's how the cat got in," Rebekah said. She tapped her chin lightly and then looked closely at the curtains.

"I don't see any claw marks," she said.

"Me either," Mouse agreed.

"There must have been a strong wind that pushed the screen out," Rebekah said. "Then the cat could climb in. He probably heard all the squeaking of the mice and-"

"Oh no Rebekah, what are you saying?!" Mouse gasped. "Do you think the cat had Magellan for dinner?" he fell back on his bed with a sigh.

"I hope not," Rebekah bit into her bottom lip. "That cat is a menace. I say we find it, and take it to the vet. She'll be able to tell if it got to Magellan."

'What a horrible thought," Mouse sniffed. "Poor Magellan."

"Don't worry," Rebekah said. "Maybe the cat just hid him away somewhere. Maybe we can still find him safe."

"Maybe," Mouse nodded a little but he did not look very hopeful. "Let's catch that cat!" he said.

They went to Mouse's kitchen and took out some supplies from the refrigerator. A little bit of turkey to tempt the cat with. A little bit of cheese in case they found Magellan and two bottles of water for them. It was going to be a long day of hunting cat.

Chapter 4

Once outside, Mouse looked everywhere for any sign of Magellan, while Rebekah looked everywhere for any sign of the cat. It was not too long before she heard the rustling again.

"Oh little kitty," she sang out. She was carrying a small cage that Mouse kept to transport his mice in. It was large enough to fit the orange cat. If they could get the cat inside of it, that is.

"Let's go this way," she said in a whisper when she heard the rustling again.

The two crept slowly toward the sound. Expecting to find the orange cat, Rebekah had her cage open and ready to catch it. Instead of catching the cat she caught a bird in the cage! It had been getting ready to take off, and when she held the cage over the leaves, it flew right up inside of it.

"Ah!" Rebekah cried out as its wings fluttered wildly.

"Ah!" Mouse shrieked as she swung the cage toward him and the bird flew out of the open door. He could feel the wind from its wings as it flew quickly away.

They both stared after the bird as it flew away, laughing and gasping for breath.

"Wow that was wild," Mouse snickered and grabbed the cage from Rebekah's hand.

"No cat in there," he said as he peeked inside the cage.

"I know, I know," she said and shrugged. 'Maybe it found a home."

Just then she saw something orange and fast streak across the street.

"Look!" she pointed at the streak. "There it goes!"

The two began to run swiftly after the cat. The cage dangled from Mouse's hand as he ran as fast as he could.

"Oh we're going to get you cat," Rebekah yelled.

The cat was very fast and could run through small spaces. It squeezed under a fence and ran off through a garden. Mouse stopped at the fence. Rebekah kept going, determined to get the cat. She did not realize she had trampled through the garden until she heard a holler from the window.

"Rebekah! Get out of my garden!" Mrs. Beasley demanded when she saw the state of her garden. "You will be replanting that!"

"Yes of course Mrs. Beasley, so sorry," she sighed. "You see there's this cat, and we think it ate Mouse's mouse."

"Rebekah, I don't care," Mrs. Beasley shook her head. "I just want my garden back to normal.

"I promise I will fix it," Rebekah said firmly and then began chasing after the cat once more.

Mouse walked around the garden and smiled apologetically to Mrs. Beasley. When they reached the edge of the yard there was no sign of the cat.

"Where did it go now?" Rebekah wondered. Then they heard a low growl from a pile of rocks beside them.

"Oh there you are," Rebekah growled back. She crouched down and motioned for Mouse to give her back the cage. He handed it over and she was ready to catch the cat inside of it. She held out the piece of turkey.

"Here kitty kitty," she called out sweetly. "Got a treat for you!" she said.

The cat inched out from behind the rocks, his head low, his back arched.

"Meow!" Mouse said, trying to talk like a cat would. Rebekah glanced over her shoulder at him with one raised eyebrow.

'What?" he said. "It might work."

Rebekah shook her head and looked back at the cat.

"One, two, three," she whispered, and then lunged forward with the open door of the cage. The cat shrieked and started to bolt, but the cage was over him before he could.

"Gotcha!" Rebekah grinned and did her best to close the cage. The cat was taking swipes with his sharp nails through the holes in the cage. He was growling long and low and hissing.

"Aw, he's scared," Mouse said. "Don't worry little cat," he said sweetly. "It's not your fault you eat mice, all cats do!"

"Don't talk to the prisoner!" Rebekah demanded. "This cat is in our custody now, and will need to stand trial."

"Trial?" Mouse gulped.

"Trial," Rebekah repeated. Then she held up the cage so she could look into the cat's little blue eyes.

"Off to the vet with this one, so we can get some hard evidence."

Chapter 5

The entire walk to the vet, the cat growled and hissed.

"What a mean cat," Rebekah shook her head.

"He's not mean," Mouse said. "He just doesn't like being in that cage."

Rebekah was swinging it back and forth mildly as she walked. She held it out far enough from her legs to keep its claws from shredding her shorts.

"If you say so she said, but it sure seems pretty mean to me."

"It has no home," Rebekah, Mouse said sadly. "I would not be very nice if I had no home, and I don't think you would be either."

"Maybe but that does not excuse mouse devouring," she said firmly. When they reached the vets office she glanced down at the cat again.

"This is it Mr. Kitty, the moment of truth. We will be able to find out from this vet if you did anything to Magellan," she paused and stared hard at the cat. "Want to make a confession now?"

The cat hissed. "Ah, a tough one I see," she clucked her tongue and carried the cat into the vet's office.

"Mouse!" the vet cried out when she saw the young boy. She knew him well as he often brought his mice in for check-ups and to see if they were eating properly.

"How are you?" she asked with a bright smile. Dr. Winston had long black hair, and big brown eyes. She had a smile that seemed to make her face glow. She was one of the nicest people in the neighborhood, according to Rebekah.

"Not so good," Mouse said as he walked up to her. "Magellan is missing."

"Oh no!" Dr. Winston said. "Well you know mice are good escape artists," she said with a frown. "I bet he'll be back in no time."

"Maybe not," Rebekah said as she plopped the yowling howling cage down on the front desk of the office.

'Who is this?" Dr. Winston asked and peered inside the cage. "Isn't this cage a little small for this cat?"

"It was all we had," Mouse said quickly.

"This is the cat that took Magellan," Rebekah said sternly. "At least, that's what we suspect."

"Oh?" Dr. Winston asked as she unlocked the cage and took the small cat out of it. She pet the orange fur soothingly and he began to settle down. He did not even try to scratch or bite her.

"Oh now you're nice," Rebekah scowled. "Don't believe it Dr. Winston this cat is just being nice so that you won't find any evidence."

"Evidence?" Dr. Winston asked with surprise.

"Yes, we are going to have a trial, and we need some hard evidence that Mr. Kitty here had something to do with Magellan's disappearance."

Dr. Winston looked very confused for a moment and then nodded slowly. "Ah, I see, evidence," she tried to hide her smile. The cat was very thin, and she knew that it needed some help.

"Let me just take a look," she said. "I will see if we can find any evidence of a mouse attack!" she whisked the cat away into the back room.

Chapter 6

Mouse sat down in one of the chairs in the waiting room and put his head in his hands. He sighed heavily.

"Poor Magellan," he said and shook his head.

"I'm sorry Mouse," Rebekah said and gave him a soft hug. "I know that you loved him very much."

Mouse sniffled and nodded.

"At least if we find out the truth we can make sure that cat gets a stiff sentence for his crime."

"Oh Rebekah," Mouse shook his head. "I don't think it would be right to punish the cat for doing just what cats do. They are built to eat mice you know, and I'm sure the cat would not have done it if he had taken the time to get to know Magellan, but that's the way animals are."

"You're too nice Mouse," Rebekah frowned and crossed her arms. "We'll just make sure the cat is somewhere that he can't hurt any more mice, how's that?"

"That's better," Mouse nodded. "Poor thing looks so sad being all alone."

"That is true," Rebekah said in a whisper. She had noticed how sad the cat looked. She remembered what Mouse had said about not being very nice if he did not have a home. He was right. If Rebekah didn't have her home and her mother and father to look after and love her, she probably would not be very nice either.

"I hope he'll be okay," she murmured.

"What did you say?" Mouse asked, as he had not quite heard her.

"Oh nothing," she said sternly. "That cat is a menace," she nodded her head sharply.

"Actually, this cat is starving," Dr. Winston said as she walked back out of the exam room. "Poor thing hasn't eaten in days."

'You mean that he didn't eat Magellan?" Rebekah said with surprise. She was sure that her theory had been right.

"Not a chance," the vet said. "His tummy was bloated from needing to eat. He's back there eating right now. It's a good thing you found him Rebekah, and brought him in. Now he will have a chance to get healthy again."

Rebekah was too shocked by the fact that she was wrong to even pay attention to what the vet was saying.

"Then where is Magellan?" Mouse asked sadly. "He's still missing," he frowned.

"I hope you find him," Dr. Winston said. "But it is a good thing this little guy got off the streets. I'll keep him here tonight and you can check on him in the morning, okay?" she smiled at the two young children.

"Yes," Rebekah said, feeling distracted. She prided herself on being a great detective and it did not feel great when she got something wrong.

"This is a good thing," Mouse said and grabbed Rebekah's hand. "This means that Magellan could still be okay. We have to find him!" he tugged her out of the vet's office. As they left, Rebecca could hear the cat's sad meow coming from the back room of the vet's office.

Chapter 7

When they got back to Mouse's house, they began to tear it apart. They looked under everything in his room. They dumped out his hamper. They turned over his trash can. They searched in the bottom of his closet, and even in the top! They looked in each one of his shoes.

"Ugh," Rebecca complained at the scent that wafted from one she peered into.

Mouse blushed and kicked his shoes back inside of the closet. They searched the bathroom. They looked in the tub, they looked under the sink, they even checked in the toilet.

"No swimming mouse here," Rebecca sighed. They headed out of the bathroom and began looking through the living room. They looked under the couch, where Mouse found an old block of cheese. They looked in the magazine rack, which was full of magazines about raising mice. They looked behind the television and found nothing but dust. They even looked in the umbrella stand.

"No mouse hiding here," Mouse sighed. "Where could he be?" he looked as if he might cry.

'Don't worry," Rebecca said. "We are going to find that mouse if it takes me all night!' she stomped one foot against the floor. She never let a mystery go unsolved.

"We just have to think a moment," she said. Her stomach began to growl. At first she thought it was the cat back in the room with them. Then she realized it was because she was hungry.

"Got any snacks?" she asked Mouse.

"Sure," he said and led her into the kitchen. "I just have to find him Rebecca," he wailed as he walked up to the tall cabinet beside the fridge. "I just can't let him be lost forever. What if he's hiding somewhere, alone and hungry? What if he's scared and lost like the cat was?"

Rebecca frowned as she thought of the cat. It was a very sad story to think about. Rebecca found herself hoping that the cat would be okay by the morning.

Mouse opened the cabinet. "Want a granola- ah!" he cried out when a little white mouse scampered across his shoe.

Well, not exactly little. Magellan's belly was round and full. Rebecca dove to catch him, but he squirmed out of her grasp. Mouse lunged into the doorway of the kitchen to keep him from getting away.

He was so happy to see the mouse he did not notice the mess in the cabinet. Magellan had helped himself to quite a few snacks while he was in there. He was an expert at chewing through cardboard. The cornflakes were all over the floor. A box of cookies had been gnawed through. He had even managed to make a hole in the bag of flour, which then trailed flour all over the floor.

Rebecca grabbed a cup from the table and ran over to where Mouse was blocking the door. She dropped the cup carefully down on top of Magellan, trapping him inside. Magellan scratched at the cup with his tiny claws and wiggled his pink nose.

"You're safe!" Mouse exclaimed happily. "I can't believe it, you're safe!"

Chapter 8

The mouse squeaked from inside the cup. Mouse slid his hand under the bottom of the cup and captured his favorite friend in the palm of his hand.

"Aw, little Magellan, you caused a lot of trouble!" he said sternly. "You shouldn't chew through your maze."

Magellan's nose twitched. He scuttled back and forth across Mouse's hand.

"I've missed you so much!" Mouse said and lifted the mouse up to look him over. He wanted to make sure that he had not been hurt while he was trapped in the cabinet. The only difference that he could see was Magellan's big round belly.

"Well you've had plenty to eat," Mouse laughed and then stopped when he looked inside the cabinet.

"Oh no, when mom sees that, she'll make me get rid of all my mice!" he groaned.

"I'll help," Rebecca offered. She grabbed a broom and a dustpan from beside the back door. Mouse returned Magellan safely to his cage and then hurried back to help too. It did not take the friends too long to get the cabinet back in shape. Of course there was no way to explain away the damaged boxes or the half-gone bag of flour.

"Just tell her the truth," Rebecca said quietly. "It's the best thing to do. She knows Magellan got loose, but you found him, and you cleaned up the mess. She'll let you keep your mice."

"Do you really think so?" he asked nervously.

"I'm sure," Rebecca nodded with a smile. They spent the rest of the afternoon playing with Mouse's mice. He decided to retire his cardboard maze and began thinking of what he could use instead. They drew some designs for a plastic maze. By the time Rebecca had to go home for dinner, it seemed like Mouse was much happier. As she said goodbye, he frowned sadly again.

"Oh no," she said quickly. "Did Magellan escape again?"

"No," he frowned. "I was just thinking that if I didn't have a home full of mice, I would give that poor kitty a home."

"Oh yes that would not be a good idea," Rebecca giggled.

"I know, I know," he murmured. "But everyone deserves a home."

"You're right," she nodded. "Maybe someone will adopt him."

"Maybe," Mouse smiled. "Thanks for all of your help Rebecca. You really are a great detective."

"You're the one that found him!" she reminded him.

"Maybe, but only because you were here to help me," he grinned.

Chapter 9

That night as Rebecca lay in her bed, she could not stop thinking about that tiny orange cat. It had been mean to her when she first found it, but she had been mean right back. It was not really a bad cat, just very sad and very lonely. She knew that if he had a home and someone to love him, he would be much happier. She went through her mind, thinking of who might like to own the cat. Maybe the older couple with the little dog. The orange cat could go on a leash too! Or maybe the mailman could use a companion. There were also the teachers at school. They might want a little kitty to go home too. But the more she thought about it, the more she knew that none of those homes would be just right for the little orange cat. He needed someone who understood what it was like to need to be loved and hugged. Rebecca felt a little different from everyone sometimes. Even though she and Mouse were friends, she didn't have too many other friends. They thought she was a little weird because she liked to solve mysteries and hunt down evidence. Rebecca knew it didn't matter what other people thought, but she did get a little lonely and sad sometimes. The poor orange cat had not found anyone to love it, and maybe he needed someone that could spend all day with him, hugging and snuggling, to help him feel loved.

"Maybe he needs me," she said in a whisper as she stared at the ceiling. "She had never even thought of taking him home with her. She had been the one to find him after all. Of course, she had never asked her parents if she could have the cat. They might not agree, since it was a stray, or because Rebecca was always so busy hunting down mysteries. But she was sure the cat could help her with that. As she fell asleep, she found herself dreaming of what it would be like to have the little orange kitty for her very own pet.

Chapter 10

The next morning she and her parents went to the vet's office to check on the cat.

"I really don't think you should have tried to catch that cat," her mother said firmly. "It could have scratched you, or bitten you, or worse. Stray animals can be dangerous and you should always tell an adult, not try to catch it yourself."

"Yes Mom," Rebecca said and bit into her bottom lip.

"Besides that, you should have called us and asked for help," her father said. "We would have helped you catch the cat in the right sized cage, and we would have made sure he was safe."

"Oh Rebecca did a very good job," Dr. Winston said as she stepped out of the back room. "She really did. If she had not caught that cat, I don't think it could have gone without food for much longer. She was very brave and knew just where to bring him for help."

Rebecca's parents smiled proudly. Her father ruffled her bright red curls.

"She is very smart," he said with a grin.

Rebecca giggled quietly.

"Let me just get him for you, so you can meet him," Dr. Winston said as she walked into the back room again. When she brought the cat back out, he was prancing on a leash. Rebecca looked at him warily. She wondered if he would try to attack her again.

"It's okay Rebecca," Dr. Winston said. "He's much nicer now. He was just so hungry and afraid yesterday. He hasn't even hissed the whole time he's been here."

Rebecca crouched down in front of the little orange cat. He purred and pushed his head against her fingertips. She smiled at how soft his fur was. She pet him carefully, not wanting to frighten him.

"See he likes you," Dr. Winston said softly. "He probably wants to thank you for helping him."

"You're welcome," Rebecca said sweetly and continued to pet him. She glanced up at her parents with wide pleading eyes.

"Oh Rebecca," her mother frowned. "I don't know."

"Hm," her father said as he looked at the cat. "So he's healthy?" he asked.

"He is, he just needs some extra meals, and he'll be just fine," Dr. Winston assured him. "We can keep him in the shelter, but he would do much better in a loving home."

Rebecca's father glanced over her head at her mother. They both looked down at their daughter being so gentle and kind to the small cat.

"Alright," her mother finally said. "But only if you promise to keep track of him and take care of him. A pet is a big job."

'I can do it!" Rebecca said happily. "I know I can!"

"So do we," her father said and hugged her. While her parents filled out the paperwork, Rebecca wadded up a tiny piece of paper and chased it back and forth across the floor with the cat.

"Rebecca, what is your cat's name?" her mother called out. She needed to write it on the paper she was filling out. Rebecca hadn't really thought about it. She had only been calling the cat one thing since she found it.

"Mr. Kitty," she said in a very serious voice.

Her parents tried not to giggle. "Mr. Kitty it is," her father said and her mother jotted down the name.

When they left the vet's office, Rebecca was the proud new owner of the meanest cat she had ever met.

Rebekah - Girl Detective #4

Ghost Hunting

Chapter 1

Rebekah and her best friend Mouse liked to do everything together. They would play kickball. They would have mice races with Mouse's pet mice. They would even investigate mysteries together. But tonight they were not doing any of that. Tonight they were watching a very spooky movie. The spooky movie was Mouse's idea of course. Mouse was curious about all things spooky. He liked aliens, and ghosts, and monsters. At least he liked to learn about them. He did not actually like to see them in person. Of course, according to Rebekah, there was no such thing as an alien, ghost, or monster, but that didn't stop them from being good friends. With popcorn to share and the lights out, they sat in Rebekah's living room.

"Is this one a zombie movie or a ghost movie?" Rebekah asked as she tossed some popcorn in her mouth.

"A ghost movie," Mouse replied as he too ate some popcorn. "It is really scary," he warned.

"It can't be that scary," she argued. "Because ghosts aren't real."

"That's what everyone says until they meet one," Mouse pointed out.

"I have never, and will never meet one," Rebekah said, standing her ground. "Ghosts are completely impossible, and there is no way that anyone can ever prove they are real," she sighed as Mouse rolled his eyes.

"Just watch the movie!" he insisted and stuffed his mouth full of popcorn. He sneaked a few pieces to the little mouse in his pocket. His pet mouse munched down on the popcorn. The mouse did not care what movie was on television. It was a very scary movie though, and by the time it was over, Rebekah was a little creeped out.

"How am I supposed to sleep now?" she asked with a frown.

"I thought you said you weren't afraid of ghosts," Mouse teased.

"I'm not," she insisted. "But I am a little afraid of people who would make a movie like this!"

The two friends laughed and said goodnight. Rebekah went to her room and crawled into bed. She was a little nervous about the lights being out after that movie, but she ignored her fear and did her best to go to sleep.

Rebekah was having a very nice dream about white rabbits. Not the white rabbits of fairy tales but actual white rabbits that were hopping all over the place. She was chasing them across a field, and every time she caught one, she would let it go just so she could try to catch another.

"Come back," she called to the rabbits. "Come back!"

Then suddenly all of the rabbits ran off, leaving Rebekah alone in the field. She noticed something out of the corner of her eye, a strange glow. It was a glow she was familiar with, but she could not remember exactly what it was. She closed her eyes for a moment to think, and when she opened them again, she was awake in her own room. She could still see the glow from her dream. In the darkness, it was really quite a scary glow.

"I'm not afraid of the dark," Rebekah said quietly as she peered toward the window. "But maybe just a little afraid of that light." The eerie glow outside of her window made her eyes open wider. She sat up slowly and looked intently out through the glass.

What she saw was more shocking than anything she could have expected. Walking past her window, as if it was not strange at all, was a woman in a white gown. It looked like she had white hair to match. In her hand was a candle. The flame flickered in the wind. She was walking very slowly. The gown was too long for Rebekah to see her feet. She could not believe what she was seeing. It was amazing, and scary. Could it be a ghost?

"Of course it's not a ghost!" she said to herself. "That movie has me going crazy!" she blinked her eyes a few times, certain that she was seeing some sort of reflection on the glass of the window. Then she looked again. There she was, still walking right across the back yard, with her candle held out in front of her.

"What in the world?"

As Rebekah pushed back her covers she saw the being continue to walk between her house and the house next door. The woman had no expression. She seemed to be staring off into the night. As hard as Rebekah tried to think of an explanation for her presence, she could not get her mind to settle down long enough to come up with a solution. All she knew for sure was that it was not normal to see a woman in a white gown walking across her yard in the middle of the night.

Then Rebekah heard a strange noise. It was a chattering sound. It kept getting louder and it was all around her. It took her a minute to realize it was her own teeth! There was no way to deny it, she was scared! She dove back under her blankets and burrowed into her pillows. She was not going to scream for her parents, but she was not going to look out the window again. As she tried to figure out how a ghost could be real, she found herself drifting off to sleep. She knew that in no time she would be ghost food, but the blankets were warm and her pillow was soft.

Chapter 2

She woke to the sound of birds outside her window. She sat up quickly, trying to decide if she was still afraid. As she sat on the edge of her bed she had another thought. Had it all been a dream? She was sure that movie had made her think up things that were not true. That was all it was. But there was still a gnawing suspicion inside of her. She decided to prove to herself, that it was no ghost that had been walking through the yard, that in fact no one had walked through the yard at all.

She slid her slippers on her wriggling toes and hurried out the back door. Her parents were still sleeping. In fact the whole neighborhood was probably still sleeping. Still in her pajamas she crouched down and looked closely at the ground. Her eyes were still a little blurry from just waking up, but she was determined to find some evidence. She was sure a real ghost would not leave footprints. The ground was moist from the morning dew. The pants of her pajamas were getting wet at the ankles from the grass. She shivered a little in the cool morning air, but ignored it.

"No ghost here," she told herself as she noticed some bent blades of grass. There was no footprint though, as if whatever had bent the grass had been hovering above it.

"Er," she sighed as she shook her head. "No, Rebekah, no way, there is no such thing as ghosts," she was certain of this. However, as she continued to study the bent blades of grass she was surprised by something strange.

"Rebekah," a voice called out in a shaky scary tone. "Rebekah, why have you left me all alone!"

Rebekah gasped and started to run backwards. As she did her shoes slid in the wet grass and she fell right down on her bottom.

"Ouch!" she sighed. She started to stand up when the bushes began to move. She froze as she stared at the bushes. Was it really the ghost? Had it come back for her?

"Rebekah, I'm sorry, are you okay?!" a worried voice asked as her friend Mouse emerged from the bushes.

"Mouse!" Rebekah huffed as she started to stand up. He reached for her hand to help her. "Why would you scare me like that?"

"Because," he tried to hide a smile. "I am usually the one that is scared, not you. I just had to take the chance to make you think ghosts might be real."

"For once," Rebekah shook her head. "I think you might be right."

Chapter 3

"Remember we were supposed to meet to go over the project for science class together?" he told her as she sighed and tried to get her heart to stop racing.

"Oh yes," she shook her head. "I forgot. I had the strangest dream, all because of that movie. But I don't really think it was a dream."

"A dream that wasn't a dream?" Mouse laughed. "Now that's a real mystery."

"It really isn't funny," she sighed as they walked back into her house. "Last night I saw something very strange."

"What was it?" he asked curiously.

"It was someone pretending to be a ghost," she replied firmly.

"Pretending?" he laughed. "How do you know they were pretending?"

"Because silly, ghosts aren't real," she rolled her eyes as if that should be obvious.

"What if they are," Mouse said. "What if you're wrong about this one?"

Rebekah lifted her chin in the air and huffed. "I am never wrong," she insisted.

"Oh really?" Mouse asked. "What about the green meat in the cafeteria?"

Rebekah sighed. "Okay, well I might have confused broccoli cuts with meat, but anyone could do that."

"Sure," Mouse laughed.

"Mouse really, there's no such thing as ghosts, you need to face that," she said firmly.

"Come with me to the library and I will show you all the books that are written on it," he said. "Maybe we can find out why a woman in a white dress would be walking through your back yard."

"Or maybe I can find all the books that prove there is no such thing as ghosts!" Rebekah said with a laugh. As they started toward Rebekah's house for her to get dressed, Rebekah noticed one of the flower pots had a small amount of water gathered in it.

"Did it rain last night?" she asked curiously.

"Very early this morning," Mouse replied. "Why?"

"Well that explains it," Rebekah said smugly. "There are no footprints, because the rain washed them away. But rain can't wash away bent grass. Our ghost definitely had feet!"

"Oh that's a relief," Mouse laughed. "I guess?" he shook his head as Rebekah ran into the house to get changed as quickly as she could. There was nothing that she enjoyed more than a good mystery.

Chapter 4

When they arrived at the library there were more cars than usual in the parking lot. Rebekah thought it was odd, but she ignored it. She was determined to prove Mouse wrong. Inside the library there was a quiet buzz of people whispering. Mouse headed straight for the shelves in the back of the library, while Rebekah headed for the science section. A few minutes later they both met up at one of the large wooden tables in the middle of the library. Rebekah had one stack of books. Mouse had his own stack of books. They sat down across from each other, ready to prove each other wrong. As Rebekah looked through her books, she heard the door to the library swing open several times.

"According to these books, the only way you see a ghost, is if they need your help," Mouse said with a frown. He was flipping through the pages of several books. They were spread out on the large table in front of him. Rebekah was looking around with some confusion at all of the people in the library. She had never seen so many people in the library at one time before.

When the librarian Mrs. Peters walked by them, Rebekah called out to her quietly. "What is going on here?" she asked. "Why are there so many people?"

"Oh it's a special paranormal group," the librarian explained. "They're showing off all of the tools they use for their investigations."

"There are tools for paranormal investigation?" Rebekah asked with a skeptical frown. "How can there be tools if ghosts aren't real?" she wondered.

Mrs. Peters smiled patiently at Rebekah. "It is good that you are so interested in science Rebekah, but it is important to remember, that no one knows everything about the world. People are entitled to different opinions about what is and isn't real," she paused as Rebekah sighed. "You should come see the tools, they are very scientific."

"See," Mouse announced proudly. "Scientific tools," he grinned as if he'd won.

"Tools for paranormal investigation," Rebekah mused as she turned back to Mouse. "Sounds like we are in luck! Let's see what they have to say about our ghost!"

Chapter 5

They headed over to the two large tables covered with the equipment that the paranormal investigators had brought with them for their speech. The two men stood at the front of the library. They had all kinds of special tools for detecting ghosts and supernatural activity. Mouse was very interested. He kept leaning closer to see the different items. Rebekah, who always admired another detective, was more interested in the way they set everything up, so they would not be detected themselves.

"For this demonstration we will need everyone to keep very quiet," the taller man said. He pointed to the librarian who was standing next to the light switch on the wall. The librarian turned off the lights, and the library was plunged into darkness. Then a faint glow began from the table where the men had their equipment set up.

"This low light will pick up on the slightest movement. If something moves, it will brighten," the man explained. "This gives our cameras a chance to get a better picture of just what is moving."

The man beside him began to speak next. "So while we are being very quiet, we also need to be very still. And maybe, just maybe, we'll get a signal that something mysterious is here with us."

Rebekah rolled her eyes. She was certain that there would not be anything mysterious in the library, at least nothing more mysterious than the two men and their strange stories.

Mouse was much more interested than Rebekah. He kept inching closer to the glow. Everyone was very quiet, and very still. That was until suddenly the light began to glow very brightly, and something white and swift bolted across the table.

"Ah!" many of the people in the crowd exclaimed. Some even knocked over their chairs. Some screamed and ran for the door. The two men who were putting on the demonstration gasped with surprise. They had not expected anything like that to happen, that was for sure.

"Wait! Wait!" the taller man said. "This is a great chance for us to show you how this works," he paused and swept his gaze over the people that were left in the audience. "Now who has an idea of what we just saw?"

"A ghost!" Mouse said as he stood up from his chair. "A real ghost!"

The two men grinned at his enthusiasm. "Maybe," one said. "Anyone else?" he asked.

Rebekah frowned as she watched the two take answers from the rest of the crowd. She wasn't sure what the blur had been, but she knew that it could not have been a ghost.

"Well let's take a look at the recording," the men suggested. "It is easy for the eyes to play tricks on the mind," he explained as he was setting up the video feed. "That is why it is so important to keep a clear mind while you investigate."

Rebekah nodded her head quickly, she could agree with them on that. She watched as the television screen flickered to life. Everyone in the crowd quieted down as they waited to see what had caused the blur. The video began to play very slowly, showing frame by frame.

"Uh oh," Mouse said as soon as he saw the first frame with the blur in it. He checked his pocket. "Oh dear," he whispered.

"What's wrong Mouse?" Rebekah asked as she continued to stare at the screen. The next frame revealed the truth.

"Mouse!" the people began to shriek. "There's mice in the library!" another person hollered. They all began to scatter for the door.

"And just who might this belong to?" Mrs. Peters asked as she walked over with a small cardboard box. "As if I even need to ask," she shook her head as she looked at Mouse. "Haven't I told you no pets in the library?"

"Sorry Mrs. Peters," Mouse said as he took the box.

"Well you two caused quite a stir," the two men laughed. "Thanks for giving us a chance to show off our tools."

They began to pack up their equipment. Rebekah was relieved that they had not been upset with them. Mouse was busy trying to contain his pet, and kept glancing over at Mrs. Peters apologetically. She was going down a list of people who had been at the library and calling them to explain why there were not actually mice in the library.

"Excuse me sir," Rebekah said, her fiery red hair making it hard not to notice her.

"Yes?" he asked with a friendly smile.

"How would you go about catching a ghost?" she asked.

"Catching one?" the two men laughed. "You can't catch a ghost, it's not really possible."

Rebekah heaved a heavy sigh. "I am talking about a ghost who is pretending to be a ghost," she said to be more clear.

"Oh," the two men exchange glances and then shrugged. "Well I guess you would have to wait for them to show up, and then take pictures or video."

The other man nodded. "If someone is pretending to be a ghost you should be able to prove it, as long as you record it," he paused and lowered his voice. "You can't dispute what is recorded. So make sure you get a good shot."

"What if it's a real ghost?" Mouse asked nervously as his mouse pet poked its head up out of his pocket.

"Listen, we do believe in ghosts," the man said. "But the truth is, it is more often a mouse than it a ghost!"

Mouse grinned sheepishly and made sure that his mouse did not escape.

"See," Rebekah said smugly as she glanced at Mouse. Mouse smirked right back.

"We'll see when we see the video," he replied.

Chapter 6

As they left the library they made plans to meet up later that night around sunset so they could stake out the ghost. As certain as Rebekah was that there were no ghosts, she still had to wonder a little. With the eerie glow of the candle and the strange way the woman had stared into the air in front of her, there was something very off about the whole situation. Besides that who would ever want to spook her in such a way? When she got home, she checked out the area where she had seen the odd figure the night before. There were still very few clues for her to rely on. She knew someone had been there, and she hoped it would not turn out to be a ghost. She did her best to keep herself busy for the rest of the day, and her mind off of the supernatural. When Mouse knocked on the front door, she was ready. She had a video camera, and a baseball bat just in case.

"What is that for?" Mouse laughed when he saw the bat.

"Just in case," Rebekah said firmly.

"In case the ghost wants to play baseball?" Mouse asked with a giggle.

"In case it's not a ghost, and she doesn't want her mystery revealed," Rebekah said in a serious tone. "If someone is crazy enough to pretend to be a ghost, then they will probably be crazy enough to attack."

"I don't know about that," Mouse frowned. "But I think it would be fun to play baseball with a ghost!"

Rebekah sighed and shook her head as she walked out of the house.

"So do you really think we can catch a ghost?" Mouse asked as he and Rebekah crept along the side of the house.

"Maybe not a ghost," Rebekah said quietly as she narrowed her eyes. "But whatever is pretending to be a ghost."

"Even after everything we learned about, and all you have seen, you still don't believe it's a ghost?" Mouse said with a sharp shake of his head. "You are a stubborn one Rebekah."

"I just think it is important to remember that there is usually an explanation for everything," Rebekah explained firmly. "Of course it is easy to say it is a ghost, and run. But it is much harder to figure out what it really is, and how we can get it to stop spooking me in the middle of the night," she added. A yawn proved that she had not been getting much sleep.

"I can't have a ghost, even a pretend ghost, prancing through my back yard in the middle of the night," Rebekah explained. She crouched down behind some bushes and pulled out her video camera. Even if she couldn't catch the pretend ghost, she was going to record it!

Rebekah checked the camera and made sure it would record. She set it up so that it would record continuously while they waited.

With the camera recording they settled back in the bushes. It would not be long before the moon was high in the sky, and the streetlights offered plenty of light from the road. It was still very spooky, since they were waiting on a ghost.

"Do you think it will see us?" Mouse asked fearfully.

"Yes," Rebekah said firmly. "And if it does, it will surely turn us into ghosts," she grinned.

"Really?" Mouse shivered. "I don't want to be a ghost."

"No silly," Rebekah laughed. "Even if it is a ghost," she paused and looked him in the eye. "Which I am sure it isn't, but even if it is, they can't hurt us right? All of the books I've read have said that they are more scared of us than we are of them,"

Mouse nodded quickly, he wanted to feel better about this, but the truth was, he thought they might be asking for more trouble than they could handle. He had brought with him his extra quiet pet mouse, Starla, who was huddled in the pocket of his jacket. He nervously fed her some cheese and crouched down beside Rebekah.

"Well I guess we will find out what we are really dealing with, as soon as the sun goes down."

"It could be awhile," Rebekah nodded. "There are a lot of ghosts, you know, ghost traffic is terrible this time of night."

"Alright alright!" Mouse laughed and glanced at her. "You are just going to tease me forever about this aren't you?" he asked

"Of course!" she replied and settled into the grass behind the bushes. She knew that they were in for a very long wait.

Even though only a few minutes had passed, it was not long before they were both startled by the sound of someone approaching.

"Who is it?" Mouse wondered as he peered through the darkness.

"It's her!" Rebekah squealed when she saw the figure step into her yard.

"Hide!" Mouse squeaked and ducked down further behind the bushes. Rebekah did too, but she kept her camera rolling.

Chapter 7

"It's no ghost at all!" Rebekah exclaimed as she crept closer to the slowly walking figure.

"What is it then?" Mouse asked through clenched teeth.

"Shh," Rebekah warned him and crept closer to the woman. She did not touch her, but walked beside her. Mouse fell into step on the other side of the woman. They followed along closely behind, careful to walk very quietly.

"Ma'am, can we help you?" Rebekah asked as she studied the woman's blank face.

She did not answer.

"Ma'am, can you tell us where you live?" Rebekah asked again, hoping for some kind of response. Again the woman just kept walking as if she didn't even hear Rebekah's voice.

"Maybe she's sick," Mouse said quietly. He still wasn't convinced that she was not a ghost.

"Let's just stay with her," Rebekah said. "Let's see where she goes."

She walked all the way across the backyard, and then paused at the fence. She turned around, and began walking right back the other way.

"She's acting so strange," Mouse frowned. "Do you think we should call for help?"

"Let's see where she's going," Rebekah said quietly. "If we go inside to call for help, she might be gone by the time we get back."

"That's true," Mouse said as they continued to walk beside the woman. She walked right down Rebekah's driveway and started to step into the street. There were two cars coming from either direction, but the woman never even checked before she put a foot down on the street.

"No!" Rebekah cried out. She grasped the woman's hand and tugged her back from the street just before the car would have hit her.

"Ma'am, didn't you see that car?" she asked. The woman didn't even blink. Now she was sure they needed to stay with her, as she was obviously not acting very safely.

The woman tried again to cross the street. Luckily this time there were no cars in her path. She walked right across to the other side and then paused for just a moment. She turned to the right and began walking along the sidewalk again. This time she almost walked right into a loose dog. The dog began barking furiously.

"Shh," Rebekah commanded without any trace of fear. Mouse had hidden behind her. The dog whimpered and ran off. Even though the dog had made such a terrible racket, the woman was still walking, and staring, just as calmly.

"This is really weird," Rebekah muttered. The woman walked past another few houses, before she turned on to a driveway. Rebekah hesitated. She did not know the people who lived in the house. She wasn't sure if they should follow.

"What do you think Mouse?" she asked. "Should we follow her?"

Before Mouse could answer, his jacket pocket rustled. The little white friend he had toted along with him suddenly escaped. It scooted across the ground right after the woman.

"I think that's our answer!" he laughed and chased after the mouse. Rebekah chased after him. They all ended up on the porch of the house, just as the door swung open.

Chapter 8

"What are you doing out here?" a surly man demanded.

"Sorry sir," Mouse said quickly as he snatched up the mouse.

"So sorry," Rebekah added as she stepped back toward the stairs.

"No, no, not you," he said in a lighter tone. "I've been looking for mother all evening, and I-" he trailed off as he looked at the woman's face. "Oh no, she's done it again!" he groaned. He blew the candle out quickly.

"Done what?" Rebekah asked curiously.

"Is she a ghost?" Mouse asked with very little tact.

"Excuse me?" the man asked with surprise. "My name is Mr. Lyle," he added as he smiled at the two children. "I'm sorry if I frightened you, or if mother did."

"No of course not," Rebekah shook her head. "I wasn't scared," she said firmly. Mouse tried not to smirk, as he knew just how scared she had been.

"You should know that she almost walked into traffic," Rebekah said calmly. "Then she almost tripped right over a loose dog."

"Oh dear," Mr. Lyle shook his head. "I'm so glad you were there, thank you for helping her," Mr. Lyle said with relief. He wrapped a blanket around the woman's shoulders to keep her warm. "My mother just moved in with us, and she has a little problem."

The woman's eyes fluttered slowly, and then opened all the way. She glanced at all the people around her with confusion.

"Where am I?" she asked with surprise.

"It's okay Mom," Mr. Lyle said. "You were sleep walking again. These kind children helped you to get back home."

"Oh dear," his mother sighed and shook her head. "I'm so sorry for causing trouble. In new places I always end up sleep walking. It's not something that I can control."

Rebekah was amazed that their ghost had turned into a sleep walking woman. She did not believe in ghosts but she never guessed that the figure would turn out to be sleep walking.

"Ma'am, you could have really been hurt," Rebekah said carefully. She didn't want to upset the woman, but she also didn't want her to get hurt. "You walked right into the street!"

"I am so lucky you kids were there," she gushed. "I just have a hard time keeping in bed when I am sleeping," she sighed. "I always have."

"Well I promise to keep an eye out for you," Rebekah offered kindly.

"And I promise to hide the candles," Mr. Lyle said. "But we will do our best to make sure that she doesn't wander off in her sleep anymore!"

After they chatted for a few more minutes, Mr. Lyle and his mother thanked them again. Rebekah and Mouse started to walk back to Rebekah's house. As they did they noticed a car stopped a few blocks ahead of them. The two men from the library had their camera out and were recording something in the trees.

"Oh maybe it's a real ghost!" Mouse said happily. "Let's go see."

"No such thing-" she gulped as Mouse grabbed her by the hand and made her run toward the two men. When they skidded to a stop beside them, Mouse was out of breath.

"What, what, are you looking at?" he asked hopefully.

"Can you see it?" one of the men asked, his eyes wide as he pointed up into the tree branches.

"What?" Mouse asked with a frown. Even Rebekah was curious as she looked up into the branches.

"The most beautiful bird I have ever seen," the other man said. All four of them looked up into the branches and smiled at the sight of a bright blue bird nestled on a branch.

"I thought it would be a ghost," Mouse said with a sigh.

"It is good to look out for the supernatural," the man with the camera said. "But it is also very important to never miss out on the natural."

Rebekah - Girl Detective #5

Grown-Ups Out To Get Us?!

Chapter 1

There was mystery afoot in Rebekah's tiny town, and she was determined to solve it. She had already been at it for a few days. It had all started when the local policeman, James Todd started handing out tickets to everyone who walked across the street. He claimed it was jaywalking and that people must cross at the crosswalk. Of course there was a brand new crosswalk too. But why? It did not lead to anywhere special, just across the street. Something seemed very strange about the fact that Officer Todd was so firm about not crossing the street.

Not only that but all of the shops along the street were cleaning their windows. They were painting their storefronts. Some had even gotten new flashy bright signs.

"Something strange is happening here," Rebekah thought as she watched another group of painters head for the last shop on the corner. Everyone was so busy, as if they were getting ready for something. Or the town just decided to freshen up and make some changes.

All of the adults she passed would stop talking as she approached, and then whisper as she walked by. She tried listening in on a few conversations but she could not seem to sneak up and go undetected. Something was very fishy and she was determined to find out what it was, even if it would mean venturing into the dark and dangerous world of the adults. All of the secrecy made her think that there was something very sinister going on.

She stopped to ask one of the teachers from the school Mr. Winston, who was speaking quietly with the owner of the hardware shop.

"Mr. Winston why is everyone acting so strange?" Mr. Winston quieted down really fast when he heard Rebekah's voice.

"Oh Rebekah," he said quickly. "Don't you have homework you should be doing?" he asked.

Rebekah stared at the teacher, her eyes wide. "Mr. Winston it's summer time."

"Oh, right," Mr. Winston scratched at the top of his head. "Well, it's never too soon to get ready for the school year. You should go home and do some review."

Rebekah gasped and shook her head. "I'm going, I'm going," she said quickly, afraid that Mr. Winston might assign her some extra summer homework. As she hurried away she heard the two men begin to whisper again. By the time she got home, she was sure that there was more than a mystery afoot, there was a plot!

Chapter 2

At dinner, her parents were extra quiet.

"I was in town today," Rebekah started to say.

"You shouldn't go into town by yourself," her father warned.

"Really Rebekah, you shouldn't be so nosy," her mother said.

"What?" Rebekah said as her fork clanged down against her plate. "I'm always allowed to go into town and I didn't even say anything about being nosy."

"Rebekah," both of her parents said at once. "Leave the grown-ups alone!"

Rebekah sat back in her chair and stared at her parents as if they had been replaced by aliens. Both were looking so sternly at her when she had not even done anything wrong. Her parents knew how much she liked to be a detective, and they had always understood. Now they were acting as if she should not even be allowed out of the house!

"Eat your peas," her father said.

"Eat more of your meat," her mother said.

But Rebekah wasn't really hungry any more.

Chapter 3

The next day Rebekah went down to the fire station to see if any of the firemen were acting suspicious too. The fire station was one of her favorite places to spend time. The firemen were always very friendly. Sometimes they would even let her take the dalmatian for a walk. When she arrived she hoped they would at least be happy to see her. In fact, they were acting very suspicious. All of the firemen were scrubbing the station and washing the fire trucks.

"What are you guys doing?" Rebekah asked with a frown. She knew it was not truck washing day, or she and her friend Mouse would have been there to help. They always volunteered to tidy up around the station and help out when the big trucks needed to be washed.

"No time to talk now Rebekah," Mitch one of the firefighters said. "We are too busy."

"But I-" Rebekah started to say.

"Go," Steve another firefighter said and pointed to the door. "We have too much to do today Rebekah, we can't talk."

Rebekah hung her head and turned away.

Discouraged, Rebekah left the fire station. She walked along the sidewalk, sniffling to herself and muttering about mean firefighters until she reached the library. Here things were just as odd. The library was getting a good power wash and new decorations in the windows. The parking lot had freshly painted lines for parking spaces. All very very odd. Mrs. Peters the librarian was standing outside of the library, watching the power washing. Rebekah stopped beside her and waited until the loud machine turned off.

"Oh it's beautiful!" Mrs. Peters clapped her hands happily.

"But why?" Rebekah asked from beside her. Because the machine had been so loud Mrs. Peters had not even heard Rebekah step up beside her.

"Oh Rebekah!" Mrs. Peters said crossly. "You should not sneak up on people!"

Rebekah sighed heavily. She was getting very tired of everyone being upset with her, just for asking a question or two. "I'm sorry Mrs. Peters," she said. "I was just wondering why the library is getting a bath."

"It was just time for a bath," Mrs. Peters said with a sparkle in her eye. "Nothing more. Now move along Rebekah, I have things to do. Much too busy today to talk."

Rebekah crossed her arms and glowered as Mrs. Peters walked away. She had never been so put off by so many people. She wondered if she had done something she could not remember. Was everyone angry at her for some reason? She decided to walk toward Mouse's house to see what he thought might be going on.

Chapter 4

As she walked further along the sidewalk she came across two men in hard hats. They were looking at a large map in their hands. It showed the main street of the town.

"What is that?" Rebekah asked curiously. She wondered if it had something to do with all of the strange activity in the town.

"Not now little girl," one of the men said and waved his hand lightly. "Far too busy right now, you must move along."

Rebekah was very surprised that they were being so rude. She was used to everyone being friendly. She decided that she had enough of the questionable activity that was going on around the town, and she would find out what was happening from a good source. Mouse would have to wait.

Beverly Bar always knew everything that was going on in town. In school, she was the person to go to when the whole world wanted to know the answer to a question. She was always the one to know it. Beverly Bar usually spent her summer days in the ice cream shop so she could catch up on all the town gossip.

This was where she was when Rebekah found her. She was sipping a chocolate shake. The first thing Rebekah noticed about Beverly Bar was that she was sitting quietly. She never sat alone. She rarely stopped talking long enough to hear the gossip she would spread. Yet today, Beverly Bar sipped her milkshake in silence.

"Beverly, what is happening around town?" Rebekah asked as she sat down beside her.

"Oh nothing," Beverly said quickly. "Nothing at all. Boring day, same as usual."

"Beverly are you feeling okay?" Rebekah asked with concern.

"Of course I am," Beverly replied and sucked down the last of her milkshake. "Sorry Rebekah I have to go. Much too busy today to talk," she hurried off out the door of the ice cream shop. Rebekah could only stare after her in shock. Beverly was certainly never too busy to talk.

Chapter 5

As the darkness fell the sounds of the town became quiet. Rebekah looked all around for anyone who might be lurking around with a can of paint. Just who was it that was painting all those new parking spaces and the crosswalk, and why? She did not see anyone with a paint can, but she did see a man speaking with the Mayor. They were standing outside one of the nice local restaurants. The mayor shook hands with the other man who wore a large top hat, and had a thin black mustache.

"Very odd," Rebekah said as she narrowed her eyes. Why was the mayor meeting with a stranger when no one else was around? Was he the one asking for all the changes in their little town? The mayor looked up quickly, and all around, as if he suspected someone was watching. But why would he worry about someone seeing him? Rebekah shivered a little as this mystery was getting very big, even for her.

As she walked home that night, her mind was filled with troubling thoughts. Was the mayor paying someone to change the whole town? If so, why? Was Officer Todd in on it as well? It seemed as if the whole town had played a part in the great mystery, everyone that was, except for the children. When she thought of this, alarm bells began to ring in her mind.

"What if they are planning something that has to do with all of us kids?" she worried. It was summer, maybe they were thinking of starting school early. Maybe they were trying to hide some new law about kids being on the main street. She couldn't think of too much trouble kids had caused lately. Why would they be left out of whatever change was happening? She still was not sure what to think as she stepped into the house for dinner. In the hallway outside of the kitchen she paused when she heard her father speak.

"Just make sure she doesn't find out," Rebekah's father's voice said clearly.

"Yes, if she does, we will have a real problem on our hands," Rebekah's mother replied. There was only so much Rebekah could take. They were hiding things from her too? She was very surprised as her parents were always honest with her, and she trusted them very much. She never expected that they would try to hide something from her.

"Oh, just think," her mother sighed happily. "Just one more day, won't it be wonderful?"

"It will," he agreed. "Finally the kids of this town will get what they deserve."

Rebekah gasped. It was about the kids!

"Hi," she said quietly as they stepped out of the kitchen. They both looked startled to see her standing there.

"Hi," her father said brightly. "Hungry?" he asked with a wide smile and held out a plate of her favorite food, spaghetti.

"Smells great!" she said at first, and then frowned. She looked from the delicious noodles up into her father's eyes. "I'm sorry," she said quickly.

"For what?" he asked with a frown.

"Just in case I did anything that I have forgotten about," she shrugged and bit into her lip. Both of her parents laughed.

"Oh Rebekah, you are a strange one sometimes."

Rebekah stared at her plate. Maybe that was why they were keeping things from her. If only she wasn't so strange.

Chapter 6

After dinner that night she crept into her room. She picked up her phone and dialed her friend Mouse.

"Mouse," she whispered into her phone. "I figured it out," she sighed.

"What?" Mouse asked sleepily. He always kept his phone beside the bed because it was fairly often that Rebekah would call in the middle of the night with some amazing story she had come up with. Rebekah told him about all of the strange activity that day. She told him how her parents had acted too.

"So now I know why," she said glumly.

"Why what?" Mouse asked with a yawn.

"Why the town is changing so much," she said quickly, "haven't you been paying attention to anything I've said?" she growled into the phone.

"Uh, most of it," Mouse replied. He tried to be supportive, but to Rebekah everything was a mystery.

"Well listen closely now," she said sternly. "I think they are trying to get rid of all of the children in the town."

"What?" Mouse asked with a short laugh. "That's nuts, even for you Rebekah."

"And just what is that supposed to mean?" she demanded.

"I just mean, that I don't think the town is trying to get rid of the children. Why would they have a playground, an ice cream shop?"

Rebekah nodded as she lay back on her bed. "It's all just a lure, trying to coax the child in, so that they can later be moved to another town. A town where children are okay."

"Oh Rebekah," Mouse frowned as he listened to how worried she was. "I think you might be a little off on this one."

"I am never off," Rebekah insisted.

"Oh really?" he laughed.

"Really," she replied.

"What about the giant purple creature?" he asked smugly.

Rebekah was quiet for a moment.

"Rebekah?" he asked.

"Well, maybe I was a little off on that one," she sighed. "But not this time!" she said firmly. "I'll be over first thing in the morning, and I will prove it!"

"Alright Rebekah," Mouse sighed and hung up the phone.

Chapter 7

"Mouse, Mouse!" she called out as she knocked on his front door. It was very early in the morning, and Mouse liked to sleep in. Instead, he woke up to the pounding on his front door.

"Mom," he said groggily as he tumbled out of bed. Then he remembered that his Mother had business in town today, so he was alone. He stumbled to the front door, still half asleep.

"What's going on Rebekah?" he asked with a groan when he saw his red-headed friend on the porch.

"There is something very strange going on here!" she said firmly.

"When isn't there?" he asked. Mouse was used to Rebekah's detective work. Most of the time it took them on wild and interesting adventures. But he did prefer them to start later in the day, especially when there was no school.

"No I mean it," Rebekah insisted. "It's like everyone in town has been replaced by pod people."

"Oh?" Mouse asked with more interest. "He liked anything that involved aliens.

"Not real pod people," Rebekah said with a frown. "Don't be so silly."

"I'm not trying to be silly," he replied. "You're the one that brought up pod people."

"Mouse!" she cried out desperately. "This is serious!"

"Okay, okay," he said. "Let me just get dressed. I'll be right back."

While Mouse was getting dressed the mailman arrived to deliver his mail. Rebekah smiled and waved at the man. He looked up at her, met her eyes, and looked quickly away. Rebekah huffed. She didn't think there was any excuse for being rude.

"I'm not going to bite," she said firmly as she walked toward the man and he walked quickly the other way.

"Sorry Rebekah, too busy to talk today!" he called out and hurried off.

"I see," Rebekah growled and put her hands on her hips.

"Rebekah did you chase off the mailman?" Mouse asked from just behind her.

"Not on purpose," Rebekah replied and shook her head.

As they walked toward town together Rebekah told him all about the strange way people had been acting.

"Well Rebekah, you do usually ask a lot of questions, maybe everyone just needed a break from it," he said as nicely as he could. "You know adults can be funny that way."

"Yes," Rebekah nodded thoughtfully. "That is true. But it seemed very odd that ALL of them are acting that way,"

"I bet everyone will be back to normal now," Mouse said and they continued to walk along.

"Maybe," Rebekah nodded a little. She wanted to believe him, but her gut told her there were a lot of secrets being kept.

Chapter 8

When they reached the main street, there was still a lot happening. Vendor carts had rolled away so that the sidewalks could be cleaned. The streets were blocked off for street sweepers. There was even a man walking around with a clipboard who seemed to be checking off different things he saw that might need cleaning or fixing.

"Hm, this is a little strange," Mouse muttered as the adults on the sidewalk hurried past them without even saying hello. As they walked by so fast, one of them dropped a pamphlet from the pile of books she was carrying. Rebekah bent down and picked it up. She tried to hand it back to the woman, but she only continued to walk as fast as she could.

"Rebekah, look at that!" Mouse said as he pointed at one of the bike racks being unbolted from the sidewalk. Two more had already been removed.

"Why are they taking our bike racks?" she wondered. Her eyes lowered to the pamphlet in her hand. It described a community called West Wood. All of the glossy pictures were filled with bright green grass, and perfect little homes. In bold text beneath one of the pictures it said, West Wood is an Adults Only community, and children are not permitted.

"Oh no!" she cried out and covered her mouth. "I knew it! I was right! But now I know why I was right! I know why they are taking our bike racks!"

"Why?" Mouse asked, still very confused.

"Because they want to turn our town into an adult only community!" Rebekah wailed as she looked around at the adults hurrying off in all directions, all doing their best to avoid Rebekah and Mouse.

"Rebekah," Mouse smacked his forehead lightly. "That is absolutely impossible."

"Maybe," Rebekah replied, and then pointed to the bold text on the pamphlet. "But why else would they be handing out these pamphlets? Why else would they be taking our bike racks, and making sure they are too busy to talk to us?"

Mouse had a hard time thinking of another reason, even though her explanation was so odd to him.

"Our parents would never allow it," Mouse reminded her firmly. "Besides, there are way too many kids in town for us all to be forced out."

"Maybe," Rebekah bit into her bottom lip. "But I for one am going to find out for sure."

Just as she spoke, she saw an entire line of children being led down one of the side streets. "Look," Rebekah said. "They won't even let those kids walk on the main street," she turned to look at Mouse, but it was not Mouse she saw.

"Rebekah, you need to go on home now," the Mayor of their small town said. Mr. Jackson was one of the most well known people in town. He had been to their school on a few occasions to speak sternly about safety, the rules of the town, and how important it was to volunteer. Rebekah had always found him to be a bit stiff, but he was the mayor after all.

"Mr. Jackson, we were just going to the library," Rebekah said nervously. Mouse stepped closer to her.

"The library is closed," Mr. Jackson said ominously. "As is the ice cream shop and all of the stores. We are doing some special deep cleaning of the main street, so we ask that everyone stay off of it."

"Everyone but the adults?" Rebekah inquired boldly.

Mr. Jackson's eyes glimmered with a strange look, but Rebekah could not tell what it meant. "Rebekah, there is no mystery here for you to solve, go on home and enjoy your day."

Rebekah stared after him as he walked away.

"Oh dear," she said and crossed her arms. "If the mayor is saying there is no mystery, then we are all in trouble!"

"This is very strange," Mouse had to admit. He glanced over at the line of children walking down the side street.

"I wonder how they will get rid of us?" Rebekah said quietly as they began to walk back toward their neighborhood. "Maybe they will put us all on buses. Maybe they will fly us to another country!"

Mouse sighed as he shook his head. "I don't know how, but I think I know when."

He pointed at a small sign on the light post they passed as they left main street.

"7PM, Bring your children!"

Nothing else. No reason why, no fancy decorations, just a simple black and white sign.

"It's going to happen tonight," Rebekah said darkly. "I can't believe this is happening."

"Me either," Mouse agreed. He had never heard of such a strange thing occurring.

"We have to find a way to stop it," Rebekah said bravely. "They can't just get rid of all the children. This is our town too!"

They agreed to meet back in town around 6:30. Until then they would have to think of a plan. How could two kids save all the kids in the entire town?

Chapter 9

That night when they met up in town Rebekah was armed with a few ideas, but she was certain none of them would work.

"What do you think we can do?" Mouse wondered.

"I think the only thing we can do, is try to talk them out of it," Rebekah sighed. "Maybe if we volunteered more, cleaned up the streets, and behaved a little better, none of this would have happened."

"No," Mouse said firmly. "This is not our fault."

They stuck to the side streets to get into town, not wanting anyone to notice them. As they walked, they heard a strange sound coming from just outside of town. It sounded like weird music, followed by very loud sounds, like stomping.

"What in the world?" Mouse asked as he looked down the street. He could not see anything yet, but it was clear whatever it was, was coming in their direction.

"Maybe that's how they plan to get all the kids out of their houses," Rebekah said with a glare. "By playing music like the ice cream man."

"Rebekah, I really don't think our parents would do this to us," Mouse said firmly.

"Maybe not, but my parents were talking about how they had to keep it secret from me, so why would they need to keep anything a secret?" she demanded. She didn't want to think it was true either. Usually she could come up with a pretty rational explanation, but this one she could not think of any other answer for. As she noticed some adults approaching she pulled mouse into an alley between two shops.

"No matter what, we have to stick together," she said sternly to him.

"Of course," he replied with a sharp nod.

The music was getting closer. The loud thumping was getting closer too. Rebekah was stunned by this, as she was sure that there was nothing that could explain it. What kind of car could have a radio so loud? Mouse was huddled close to her as they both tried to figure out what was happening.

All of the sudden all of the shops on the street turned on their lights. It was late afternoon and nearly closing time for most of them. What were they doing lighting up the street?

"Oh no, something is definitely happening," Rebekah said as she saw the adults beginning to flood the streets. They all had their children in tow.

"It's happening!" Rebekah squealed and grabbed Mouse's hand. "We have to hide, we have to find a place where no one will see us!"

Mouse was very confused. He was sure that Rebekah was wrong on this one. Why would their parents turn them over? But all of the children in town were being led out to the sidewalks. They all looked as confused as Mouse felt. His own parents arrived not long after, looking for him.

"Mouse?" they called out through the crowd.

"Don't answer," Rebekah commanded. "If they find us, we'll be toast!"

Mouse stayed quiet and sniffled.

"Rebekah!" she heard her father call out over the noise of the people gathered on the street.

"Dad?" Rebekah whispered quietly. She did not want to believe that her parents would want to give her away either. What was so wrong with having kids in a town? They kept everyone smiling. They always made sure grass was mowed and leaves were raked. They were a lot of fun to have around.

The music that was approaching was very lively. It did not sound like the kind of music you would expect from something arriving to take all of the children in town away. Rebekah was curious when she began to hear the other children cheer.

"What is happening?" Mouse wondered as he peered around the edge of the alley.

"I'm not sure," Rebekah replied and also tried to see around the corner. She did not want to be tricked, but that music sounded like a lot of fun. Just as she was peering around the corner she heard the roar of a lion!

"Ah!" she cried out and ducked back into the shadows. "They brought lions!" she squealed.

"Lions?" Mouse had to see. He stepped out of the alley and gasped with surprise.

"Rebekah, come look," he said quickly. "Come see, hurry!"

With all the cheering, and even Mouse seeming very excited, Rebekah decided to take a look. She didn't see anything at first, until the first big elephant came pounding through!

"An elephant?" she said with surprise.

"They're not here to take us away," Mouse laughed. "It's a circus!"

"A circus?" Rebekah was shocked. "How, why?" she sputtered. Her mother stepped up beside her.

"Rebekah our whole town is so proud of all of our kids, we just wanted to plan a special surprise for them."

"A surprise?" Rebekah laughed. "Why didn't you just tell me?"

Rebekah's parents exchanged a long glance. "Well Rebekah, we weren't sure you would play along and keep it a secret, like Beverly."

"Beverly knew?" Mouse asked with a frown.

"Of course she did," Rebekah laughed and threw her hands up in the air. "Beverly knows everything!"

Chapter 10

They all followed along, watching the parade as it marched down Main. It was a beautiful sight to see, from the wild animals, the dancing clowns, and the flipping acrobats. The musicians were filling the entire town with music. The children were happily running along beside the circus. Rebekah had to admit that she had certainly been wrong about this one. She was happy to be wrong.

When the circus pulled into the fairgrounds, it did a slow circle before stopping. The Ringmaster, the man who Rebekah had seen talking to the mayor, stepped forward. Mr. Jackson soon joined him.

"When your Mayor told me what wonderful kids he had in his town, we knew we had to put on a special show just for you!" he waved his hand and the acrobats tumbled around in front of him. "So before we open tomorrow, all the children of the town get a front row free show!"

All of the children cheered with excitement. Rebekah was jumping up and down along with Mouse. Before they went in to see the show, Rebekah's father pulled her gently aside.

"What were you thinking we were planning?" her father asked as he looked closely at Rebekah. He knew that she had suspected something bad.

"Maybe that everyone decided that the town would be better off without kids," Rebekah cringed.

"Oh Rebekah," her father laughed. "You have some imagination," he hugged her tightly.

"You sure do," her mother grinned and hugged her. "Don't you know how important you are to us? How important all of the kids here are to the town?"

"I do now," Rebekah giggled and blushed over how wrong she had been.

Chapter 11

That night she learned two important things. One, her parents would never ever try to send her away. Two, sometimes it was a very good thing to be wrong.

She settled in beside Mouse, to watch the show. As the lights of the tent dimmed and the animals began to call out, she noticed Mouse squirming.

'What's wrong?" she asked, narrowing her eyes. "Sit still!"

"I can't," he squeaked, or at least she thought he squeaked. Until she saw all the little pink noses poke up out of his pockets.

"Mouse!" she said with surprise. "How many do you have with you?" Mouse had a huge collection of mice, and he usually had one or two tagging along, but never this many.

"Well, I didn't know what would happen," he frowned. "I didn't want to leave them behind."

"Oh Mouse," Rebekah giggled as he tried to keep all of the mice from squirming out of his pockets.

"At least they get to see the show too," she said with a bright smile.

"Yes, pay attention mice," Mouse said. "Because next, we're going to figure out how to put on a mouse circus!"

Rebekah - Girl Detective #6

The
Missing Gems

PJ Ryan

Rebekah - Girl Detective #6

The Missing Gems

Chapter 1

Rebekah was headed off to a very special field trip. She and her best friend Mouse, who was not a mouse at all, but a boy who liked to keep mice as pets, were going to visit the history museum in the city. Rebekah's teacher Mrs. Morris was in charge of their group, which made Rebekah even happier. Mrs. Morris was one of the nicest teachers she knew. Rebekah's normally loose and curly red hair was braided tightly, and she was wearing her very best attempt at an archaeologist's uniform which included khaki pants and a button down khaki top. She topped it off with a hat from her old dress up kit.

"You do know we're just going to visit, right?" Mouse asked her as he sat beside her on the bus.

"What do you mean?" Rebekah asked innocently.

"I mean, you can't actually do any digging at the museum, you can only look at what has already been found," he pointed out. As one of the teachers walked down the row counting off the students, he covered up his shirt pocket, where one of his mice was hidden. Mouse always had one of his pets with him. Today he had brought along Arthur, who of course was named after the famous archaeologist Arthur Evans.

"Oh Mouse," Rebekah sighed and wiggled one of her hands through the air. "There is always something new to be discovered!"

"Oh no," Mouse groaned as he sank down in his seat. Rebekah was their town's best detective; at least she liked to think so. She was always investigating something. Usually those investigations involved Mouse getting into some kind of hot water. But Rebekah always solved her mystery!

Rebekah scooted forward in her seat and smiled over the next seat at the kids that were sitting in front of her.

"Isn't it amazing to think that once there were no cars on this road?" she asked with a smile.

"What's even more amazing is the invention of seat belts," Mrs. Morris said as she pointed to the belt that Rebekah had neglected to fasten.

"Sorry," she blushed and clicked her seat belt shut. "I'm just really excited about the museum."

"Me too," Mrs. Morris winked and then returned to her seat. The bus ride was a long one, and the teachers kept the kids busy singing songs and telling round robin stories. Each student had a turn to add their own spin to the story that was being passed around the bus. When it came to Rebekah's turn, everyone quieted down and listened closely to what she would add. So far the story was about a brown robin that got lost in the jungle and barely made it through a patch of marshmallow goo before climbing on to a rocket ship and being shot off to the moon, which the rabbit soon discovered was made out of lettuce, not cheese!

"So the brown rabbit munched a hole right through the lettuce moon and in the middle it found-" Rebekah started to say.

"The museum!" some of the other students started to cheer. As much as the kids liked to hear Rebekah's ideas, they were too excited by arriving at the museum to hear the end of the story.

"I'm listening," Mouse grinned at Rebekah. "What did the rabbit find?"

Rebekah smirked and winked one green eye. "The museum of course!"

Chapter 2

As the students piled off the bus, the teachers did their best to keep them in an orderly line. Mouse had shifted Arthur to his book bag front pocket so that he would not be spotted.

"Don't scratch my camera," he warned as he added a crumble of cheese to keep Arthur quiet. When they made it into the museum they were divided into groups. Rebekah hoped they would get to stay with Mrs. Morris, but instead they had to join a group led by Mrs. Konti. She was the strictest math teacher that Rebekah had ever had! When Rebekah wore sandals to school and tried to make a joke of counting her fingers and toes, Mrs. Konti warned her that she would get detention if she kept it up. She took math very seriously. It seemed to Rebekah that Mrs. Konti took everything very seriously.

"Now children," she said sternly. "I don't want any of you running off. We must stay together as a group, and do not touch anything!" she stamped one foot to make that last point clear.

Rebekah sighed, and Mouse patted the front of his book bag. "That means you Rebekah," Mrs. Konti said with a nod of her head.

"Yes Ma'am," Rebekah replied and frowned. She did not like to be singled out. But Mrs. Konti had a point, since she had been the one to leave fingerprints all over the computer screens in their new computer lab. Rebekah found it to be very interesting and thought she could use the screens as a way to record fingerprints. She had spent an entire afternoon wiping the screens clean while being lectured about the cost of the flat screen monitors.

Chapter 3

The tour guide that would lead them through the museum stepped up. He was a tall and thin man wearing tiny little glasses that perched on the end of his narrow nose. He looked a bit miffed to be leading the group in the first place.

"Hello children," he said and offered a small smile. "Our tour begins with-" as he began to speak about the first display, Rebekah's attention wandered. She had learned that being a good detective meant paying attention to what no one else noticed. So when everyone was looking in one direction, she tended to look in another. There in the window, not far from where they stood, was an empty pedestal. She narrowed her eyes so that she could read the description from a distance. It was supposed to be a collection of gems. But the gems were missing! Rebekah tugged at Mouse's sleeve, but he waved her away. He was trying to hear the speech about the dinosaur bone on display in the window right in front of them.

"Mrs. Konti," Rebekah called out, trying to get her teacher's attention.

"Shh!" she said sharply to Rebekah and gave her an annoyed look.

Rebekah pursed her lips and raised her hand. She waited, hoping that either her teacher or the tour guide would call on her. But Mrs. Konti was standing just in front of her, blocking her from view. The group began to move on to another section of the tour. Mouse was following, until Rebekah grabbed his book bag and pulled him backward.

"Mouse, please," she said. "I have to show you something!"

"What is it?" Mouse asked as he adjusted his book bag and got his balance.

"Look, the gems in this display are missing!" she said with a frown.

"Oh no," he tilted his head slightly to the side. "Are you sure they're not just invisible?"

"Of course they're not invisible," Rebekah said with a sigh. "The sign doesn't say anything about them being invisible."

"Oh," he nodded a little. "Well, I'm sure they'll turn up."

"No they won't," Rebekah said firmly. "Not if we don't find them."

"Rebekah," Mouse sighed. "We can't get in trouble today, okay?"

"Trouble?" Rebekah crossed her arms. "I suppose ignoring the theft of gems would be okay, as long as we don't get into trouble?"

"Right," Mouse nodded sharply and started to walk back toward the group.

"Mouse, get back here!" Rebekah demanded. "I need your camera to take pictures of the evidence."

Mouse turned back with a sigh. Rebekah was his best friend, and he wasn't going to let her get into trouble without him, that was for sure.

"Here, just get it out of my bag," he said and turned around so that she could unzip it. Rebekah pulled out the camera. She scrunched up her nose as she brushed off a few tidbits of cheese.

"What are you going to take a picture of?" Mouse asked. "There's nothing there."

"I'm going to take a picture of what isn't there," she replied with a smile. She snapped the photograph. Then she flipped the camera over and using the tools, she expanded the picture so that it was much larger than even the naked eye could see.

"Look," she pointed to the indents in the cushion that would have held the gems. "Now we can see what size they were, so that if we spot someone with them, we will know if they are the right ones."

"Good thinking!" Mouse exclaimed and smiled proudly at Rebekah. Even though it wasn't always easy to be swept up into her mysteries, it was always fun!

"Now we just have to figure out who took them," Rebekah said sternly. "If the museum staff won't listen, then we will have to do their job for them."

Chapter 4

The two set off down the hallway while their tour group got further and further ahead. Rebekah stalked a few steps in front of Mouse, her eyes seeking out the tiniest details about the people that she saw milling about. What her close observation could not reveal was the fact that she had not zipped up Mouse's book bag after she had opened it, which meant that there was a little mouse on the run!

They walked up to one of the displays where many people were gathered. A museum staff member was reaching inside to point out the different aspects of the ancient artifacts inside of the window. When the crowd began to gasp and shriek, Rebekah knew that something strange was happening. She and Mouse pushed politely to the front of the crowd. Rebekah's eyes widened and Mouse groaned when they saw Arthur scuttling across the artifacts.

"Oh no! I knew I was going to get into trouble!" Mouse sighed. Arthur ran right back out of the display, making people jump and run away from the tiny animal. Mouse chased after him, but he managed to get into a sandy exhibit of what it was like for explorers to cross the desert. There was no way for him or Rebekah to get into the display, so Arthur was on his own to cross the desert. Luckily it was only a few feet wide, and he made it to the other side. While everyone was gasping and trying to hide from the mouse, Rebekah was still watching very closely. She noticed that one man, instead of looking at the mouse, or the people who were scared, began to walk down a side hallway.

"Look Mouse," she hissed as she watched the man glance over his shoulder and then hurry down the hallway. "That man looks like he's up to something."

"Little busy here," Mouse called out as he lunged forward, trying to capture Arthur before he got to the dinosaur display. He failed, and the white mouse scooted off across the carpet and right into the dinosaur display.

"Oh please, please, don't let him knock it over!" Mouse squeaked and fumbled for the cheese in his book bag. The little white mouse was running around the boney feet of the dinosaur skeletons. Each time he brushed along the bones, the skeleton shivered. "Look Arthur, cheese!" he called out. The mouse sniffed the air for a moment. Then he set his beady eyes on the cheese. He ran toward it, evading the sight of one of the museum staff members. Mouse scooped him up swiftly and tucked him safely back into his book bag with the cheese. Then he tried his best to look as if he knew nothing about mice.

"Mouse!" Mrs. Konti called out, her eyes narrowed into a glare. "You didn't happen to bring any of your pets with you today, did you?"

"Of course not Mrs. Konti," he said with a small smile. "Bringing a mouse to a museum, that would be silly."

'Yes it would," Mrs. Konti agreed. "You two keep an eye out, okay?"

"We will Mrs. Konti," Rebekah agreed. "Oh!" she gasped and pointed down the hallway. "I think I see something down there, can I go check?"

Mrs. Konti looked back at the chaos that the museum had fallen into while the mouse was on the loose, then she nodded to Rebekah.

"Okay, but no getting into trouble!"

Rebekah sighed. "Why does everyone tell me that?" she asked.

Mouse laughed and they walked down the hallway together.

"I saw him go in one of the doors," Rebekah whispered. "We have to hurry, we won't have much time. If Mrs. Konti thinks we're gone too long, she'll come looking."

"Do you really think he's the one who took the gems?" Mouse asked with a frown.

"He looked like he was up to something," Rebekah said with a nod.

"Rebekah, you think everyone is up to something," Mouse reminded her. Rebekah opened her mouth to argue, but she had no ground to stand on. He was right. She had once questioned a fireman about why he was loitering beside a hydrant. It had seemed suspicious to her at the time.

"Here, this door," Rebekah whispered. She paused beside it. There was a small rectangular window in the door. She peered through it. Inside was a small office with a table and a bright adjustable light. The man was hunched over the table, mumbling to himself.

"See, he's talking to himself," Rebekah pointed out. "Very suspicious."

"Sure," Mouse shook his head and peered through the window. "Oh Rebekah look!" he said when he pointed to a mirror that was on the desk. In its reflection he could see the assorted gems. They were different sizes and many different colors, but they were the right shapes for the indents they had taken a picture of.

"The gems!" Rebekah said happily. "We've found them!"

"Now what?" Mouse frowned. "We can't exactly ask him for them back."

"Why not?" Rebekah shrugged her eyes narrowed with determination.

"Rebekah, if he's stealing the gems, then he's a dangerous man!" Mouse said firmly. "We can't just accuse him of a crime. We're just kids and he won't listen to us!"

"You're right," Rebekah sighed and shook her head. Then she noticed another doorway marked storage. She smiled to herself. "But maybe, just maybe, if we weren't just kids."

'What do you mean Rebekah?" Mouse asked and winced.

Chapter 5

Rebekah stepped over to the storage closet and tried the knob. Luckily it was unlocked. She had been to the museum before, and knew that during Halloween they had some very funny decorations. Whether they would be in this closet or not she wasn't sure, until-

"Ah! What is that?" Mouse cried out as he ducked back out of the closet. In the very back of the closet, half hidden by the shadows, was a mummy dummy.

"Don't worry it's just a dummy," she said with a grin and reached out to grab it.

"Don't touch it! Don't touch it!" Mouse squeaked. It looked very real. But when Rebekah picked it up, it was very light.

"They use these at Halloween as a joke," she explained and showed it to Mouse. "It's as harmless as a teddy bear."

"Hmph, I like my teddy bears to look like bears," he said sharply.

"So you have teddy bears?" Rebekah grinned.

"Rebekah!" Mouse sighed and shook his head.

"Come on, let's see if this will work," Rebekah smirked. She held the dummy out in front of her and spoke in a booming voice. "Mouse, do I sound like a mummy?" she asked.

"Oh stop," he laughed. "I'm not sure whether to laugh or run!"

"So it will work?" she asked as she peeked around the shoulder of the mummy.

"I don't know Rebekah, but it sure is spooky," Mouse nodded.

Rebekah frowned. "Well it's worth a try I guess," she said and together they carried the dummy out of the storage closet.

"Now you knock on the door and get his attention, then run off. Go back to Mrs. Konti so she doesn't come looking for us. Tell her I went to the bathroom, okay?"

Mouse nodded, but he frowned. "Rebekah what if he doesn't believe you? What if he gets angry?"

"I'm not afraid," Rebekah said firmly.

"I don't know, if he's a thief," Mouse shook his head. "Maybe this isn't such a good idea."

"I'll be fine," Rebekah promised. "If you don't hear from me in twenty minutes, then tell Mrs. Konti what happened, okay?" she asked. They both checked their watches to make sure they were set for the same time.

"Be careful Rebekah," Mouse said as he started to walk off. Rebekah made the dummy mummy wave its hand at him.

Mouse shivered and grimaced. "Stop!" he pleaded and walked back to the door where they had seen the man hunched over the gems. He knocked loudly on the door. Then he waited to make sure that the man was getting up. Then he ran off down the hallway to rejoin the school group, which was still teamed up with the museum staff to try to catch the mouse. Luckily Arthur was safely tucked into Mouse's book bag.

Chapter 6

When the man opened the door to the office and peeked out curiously, Rebekah went into action. She raised the mummy dummy up in front of her and waited until he looked her way. When she heard him gasp, she began to bellow.

"You have stolen ancient gems! You must give them back! You must not steal them!" she said in a voice so loud and so dark, that the man shuddered.

"Ah!" the man was startled by the sight of the mummy dummy. Then he wagged his finger. "Who is back there?" he asked. "You shouldn't be playing with that!"

Rebekah had to think fast. The man didn't believe she was a mummy. If she didn't get to the gems, he was going to get away with stealing them! So she shoved the mummy toward the man and bolted into the room where the gems were.

"Hey!" the man shouted as he tried to get the mummy out of his way. "Just what do you think you're doing?" he demanded. Rebekah snatched up the gems and ran right back out of the office.

"Stop!" the man shouted.

"You'll never steal these gems!" she shouted back and ran toward the door at the end of the hallway.

"Wait! Come back!" the man pleaded and chased after her.

Rebekah reached the end of the hallway. She glanced around quickly. There was an emergency exit that she knew would set off alarms if she ran through it. So many times she had been told by teachers and other adults not to push on those doors, they were not toys! But today, she had no choice. She had to get away and get the gems safely back to the museum staff. When she pushed on the door and swung it open, she heard the man's footsteps running behind her.

"Stop right there!" he bellowed.

Chapter 7

Inside the museum Mouse heard the alarms go off. He cringed and knew that Rebekah's plan had not worked out the way she wanted it to. He checked his watch, but it had only been ten minutes. He had promised he would not tell Mrs. Konti until twenty minutes had passed. The children and staff were still looking for the mouse when the alarms began to ring.

"Alright children, stay calm," Mrs. Konti said and held her hands up into the air. "We are going to have to evacuate the museum, so please line up."

Of course the students who were already hyped up over the mouse and stunned by the sounds of the alarm did not get into a straight line. They started running in all different directions!

"No! No! Come back!" Mrs. Konti cried out. Now the museum staff was busy gathering up students and getting them into a line, while the other patrons of the museum began walking out into the parking lot.

"Is there a fire?" one woman asked another.

"Has there been a theft?" a man asked one of the museum staff.

"We don't know sir," the staff member said. "But it is best if everyone evacuates the building until it can all be sorted out," he said. "Maybe that pesky mouse has something to do with it!"

Mouse checked the pocket of his book bag to make sure Arthur was still there. He sighed with relief when he saw him nibbling on a hunk of cheese. As they began leaving the museum, Mouse looked over his shoulder. He hoped that Rebekah was okay.

Chapter 8

Rebekah was not okay. She was being chased by the gem thief! She had hoped he would give up once she got out the door, but he was right on her heels! Rebekah ran as fast as she could across the parking lot. She knew she shouldn't leave the museum with the gems, but she was sure the staff would understand when she returned them safe and sound. With the gems clutched tightly in her hand she continued to run as swiftly as she could.

"Young lady stop this instant!" the man shouted after her.

"You'll never get these gems!" she shouted back over her shoulder. But he was not slowing down. He was running very fast, and catching up! She was almost at the end of the parking lot, and the alarms were blaring in the museum. She cringed as she wondered how Mouse was handling things inside. She didn't have much time to think about it, as she could hear the man's footsteps getting closer!

Chapter 9

She didn't notice as the entire museum began to empty out into the parking lot. Mrs. Konti was counting off the students in her group, when she gasped in horror.

"Oh no! One is missing!" she cried.

Mouse winced. "Oh Mrs. Konti, Rebekah was using the bathroom!" he said quickly.

"Oh dear, oh no," Mrs. Konti was very frazzled. She waved to one of the museum staff members. "We still have a child inside!"

"Don't worry," the staff member assured her. "We have people clearing each room and the restrooms. If she is inside we will find her."

Mouse frowned as he wondered what would happen when they discovered that Rebekah wasn't inside the museum.

"Maybe she went back inside," he thought, and then glanced over his shoulder. In the distance running across the grassy field, he spotted Rebekah's red braids.

"Oh no!" he groaned as he saw the gem thief chasing after her. "Run Rebekah!" he shouted.

His shout made the other students see what was happening, as well as the teachers.

"Look!" one of the kids shouted. "Where's Rebekah going?"

"Rebekah!" Mrs. Konti and Mrs. Morris screamed at the same time.

Rebekah heard her name screamed across the grass, but she kept running. She knew if she let the man catch her, she might never be able to keep the jewels safe. When the museum staff saw the scene unfolding they weren't sure what to do at first.

Then they saw the man chasing after Rebekah, and they went right into action. The security staff began charging after Rebekah and the man she was running from.

When she heard the sound of more footsteps behind her, she glanced over her shoulder. She was relieved to see that the security was coming. They would be glad that she had kept the jewels safe. She also saw that the man chasing her was getting tired. He was not running nearly as fast as he had been. His cheeks were very red, and he was huffing and puffing. The security staff was getting closer. At the edge of the parking lot, their tour guide stood with his hands on his hips and his eyes narrowed behind his glasses.

"Is that one of your students?" he demanded. "Has she stolen something from the museum?"

"Of course she hasn't," Mrs. Konti said sharply. "Rebekah may cause mischief, but she is not a thief!"

"Well we'll see what security has to say about that," the man replied with a snarl.

Chapter 10

Mrs. Konti did not want to let Rebekah get into trouble for something she didn't do. She reached into her large purse and pulled out her sneakers. She changed quickly from her dress shoes into her sneakers and bolted across the grass. Mrs. Konti ran marathons. She was a track and field star when she was in high school. Mrs. Konti outran the security staff.

"Rebekah!" she shouted. Rebekah's eyes widened as she heard the voice. She knew that she was in real trouble now. But she was sure that once the teacher heard about how she had foiled a gem theft, everything would work out just fine. At least she hoped so. Rebekah was so busy looking over her shoulder at Mrs. Konti that she tripped over a rock in the grass.

"Oh no!" as she fell her hands opened up, and the gems she had been carrying scattered into the grass.

"Rebekah!" Mrs. Konti said with a frown.

"Young lady!" the gem thief growled.

"What is going on here?" the security staff demanded.

"Get him!" Rebekah announced. "He stole gems from the museum!" she pointed at the man standing over her.

"I didn't," he panted. "I didn't steal anything!"

The tour guide and some other members of the museum staff had caught up in time to hear Rebekah's accusation.

"That's John Reynolds, he's our gem expert," the tour guide said with a frown. "He didn't steal any gems."

"But, but," Rebekah stammered. "They were missing from the display and then I saw him with them," she frowned.

"Of course you did," he said as he stumbled back toward her. "I was cleaning them. Some dust had collected on them and they were losing their luster, so I was cleaning them to make them nice and shiny for the field trip. I had hoped to have them ready before you left," he sighed and drew a deep breath.

Rebekah looked up at all of the adults glowering down at her. She arched a brow and tried a small smile, hoping that she could charm them into understanding that it was all an innocent mistake.

"Sorry?" she said hopefully.

"Sorry for nearly giving Mr. Reynolds a heart attack?" the tour guide asked.

"Sorry for setting off an emergency alert with the security staff?" one of the security men asked.

"Sorry for causing such a disaster on our field trip?" Mrs. Konti asked.

"Sorry, I dropped the gems," she winced and started sifting through the grass.

"The gems!" everyone gasped.

"I was just trying to help," Rebekah sniffed as she looked through the grass.

Chapter 11

Everyone started to look with her. It wasn't too long until they had collected all of the gems but one. Rebekah searched and searched.

"Here it is!" she suddenly called out and picked it up off the ground. When she did she brushed some dirt aside from something else on the ground.

"Let's go Rebekah," Mrs. Konti said with a sigh of relief as she handed the last gem to Mr. Reynolds.

Rebekah was too busy with her new mystery to answer. She looked down at what she had found closely.

"Look at this," she said quietly.

"Enough mysteries Rebekah!" Mrs. Konti said.

"No, it looks interesting," Mr. Reynolds said as he eyed the piece. "It looks like a piece of a clay pot."

Other museum staff members began gathering around Rebekah and Mrs. Konti.

"Oh she's found it!" one of the staff members cried out.

"What do you mean?" Mrs. Konti winced, hoping that Rebekah had not caused any more trouble.

"We knew that this once was the location of an Indian tribe," the tour guide explained. "It was one of the reasons the museum was built here. But we've never been able to find any evidence of the lost tribe. Now this," he sighed as he crouched down in front of the piece of the clay pot. "This is amazing!"

Rebekah smiled a little. Mrs. Konti arched a brow. Rebekah stopped smiling.

"What happened here today was very serious Rebekah," she said firmly. "You caused a lot of trouble with your mischief."

Rebekah lowered her eyes. "I know," she sighed. "I really didn't mean it."

"I know you didn't Rebekah," Mrs. Konti smiled a little. "But you could have just told me about it."

"I tried to," Rebekah protested.

"Next time, try harder!" Mrs. Konti said. "This was supposed to be the best field trip of the year. It's time to head home Rebekah and now we'll never get to see the museum," Mrs. Konti sighed as she glanced at her watch.

"Well, since you missed your field trip, and without Rebekah's antics we never would have found this site, how would you and your students like to assist us in excavating the site?" the tour guide offered. "I am sure the owner of the museum would agree to it."

"Oh can we?" Rebekah pleaded as she looked up at her teacher. She was sure Mrs. Konti would say no. She always seemed so serious. It was only then that Rebekah noticed the sneakers peeking out from Mrs. Konti's skirt. Maybe there were a few things she didn't know about this teacher.

Mrs. Konti couldn't help but smile and shake her head. "Of course we can Rebekah."

Over the next few months the students were able to visit the site once a week and assist in uncovering the artifacts of a lost Indian tribe. They found items that were used to cook with and some tools. It was the first evidence of the tribe living on the land that the museum had purchased. It drew visitors from all over the world to observe the excavation.

186

"I guess you were right, as usual," Mouse muttered as they sifted through some dirt.

"Right about what?" Rebekah asked curiously.

"There's always something to discover," he laughed.

Rebekah - Girl Detective #7

Swimming With Sharks?!

Chapter 1

One of Rebekah's favorite times of year was summer. Not just because school was out, which meant no homework, there were other reasons too. The sun stayed out longer, giving her plenty of time to investigate. There was always an ice cream truck around the corner. Sometimes her family would eat dinner out back under the stars. But her favorite part of summer, hands down, was spending the day at the lake. The lake was not far from her house and had a sandy beach to play on. The water was always cool and easy to splash in. During the summer she and some of her friends from school would meet up at least once a week to go swimming together. It was something she looked forward to.

This week was a very special week because Rebekah was going to swim under the water for the first time. Rebekah liked to swim, but she didn't like putting her head under the water very much. She was just a little bit scared to do it. Mouse had shown her dozens of times that it was easy, but she still didn't want to try.

After seeing one of her friends dive under the water and come back up with a big rock, she decided she wanted to be able to investigate under the water too! So for the first time she was going to be brave about this underwater business. She was finally ready to put her head under the water!

Of course she had to make sure she had the proper equipment that she needed in order to succeed at her underwater journey. She had the perfect swim cap! She was able to tuck all of her red curls under it. It was a little snug, but at least her hair would be safe.

She also had a brand new pair of swimming goggles, so that she could see under the water. Rebekah didn't like to miss anything and this was the main reason she wanted to take on this mission. She imagined there might be a sunken ship, or some lost treasure, or even fossils of ancient animals hidden beneath the surface of the lake. It was too exciting not to take a look!

Chapter 2

When she arrived at the lake her best friend Mouse was already there. He was busy beside the edge of the lake setting up what looked like a miniature swimming pool.

"Mouse? Did you bring your dolls to the lake?" she asked with surprise as the pool looked just like the one she had for the little dolls she still liked to dress up and play with.

"No," Mouse shook his head and smiled. "It's not for dolls!" He reached into his pocket and pulled out one squirmy white mouse. This was how Mouse got his nickname. He didn't look anything like a mouse, but he had several mice as pets. He always had one with him, sometimes more than one. In the little pool he had placed a pile of sand, a little lounge chair and small bowls of food and water.

"Why should I get to have all the fun?" he asked with a grin. He put the mouse gently into the pool. "Little Lochness here needs a day in the sun too!"

"Lochness?" Rebekah rolled her eyes at the name that Mouse had chosen for his pet. "Are you serious?"

"Well sure," Mouse shrugged. "We're at a lake, it seemed like Lochness would be the right mouse to bring along. He is named after a famous lake monster after all."

"Oh Mouse, there are no such things as lake monsters," she shook her head and placed her hands on her hips.

"There might be," Mouse said firmly. "There have been a lot of sightings, pictures, and stories, about strange creatures that lurk in the depths of lakes all around the world!"

"Stories would be the key word," Rebekah said with a smirk. "Because they are made up, like fairy tales. They're just little stories people tell each to scare one another."

"If you say so," Mouse shrugged and dropped some cheese into the pool for Lochness. "But one thing is for sure, if there is a lake monster in our lake, I'm going to get proof!" he held up his waterproof camera. "So we'll see what you have to say when I get my photograph!"

Chapter 3

Rebekah and Mouse splashed into the water. It was a little chilly but the heat from the sun warmed them up real fast. Mouse tried out his camera by dunking it into the water and then snapping a picture. He smiled when it still worked.

"Are you really going to put your head under the water today?" Mouse asked Rebekah.

"Yes, I think it's time," Rebekah said proudly. Most of her friends already knew how to swim under the water. Rebekah's mother had once asked her if it made her feel bad that she couldn't do what her friends were doing in the water. Rebekah had only shrugged.

"When I am ready to put my head under the water, I will," she said confidently.

Now she was ready. At least, she thought she was. She pulled her goggles down over her eyes and blinked a few times at Mouse.

"How do I look?" she giggled.

"You look like you just might be the lake monster!" Mouse laughed and then swam away as quickly as possible.

"Oh I'll show you a lake monster!" she shouted and swam after him, careful to keep her head above the water. When they reached a point of the lake where Rebekah's toes could barely touch the sandy floor, she stopped. This was usually as far as she went in the water. She didn't feel so confident swimming, since she didn't swim under the water.

"Today is the day," she told herself confidently.

"Just count to three, and dunk!" Mouse told her. "Watch me," he grinned and held his nose. "One, two, three!" he said in a nasally voice. Then he plunged beneath the water with a big splash. Rebekah wiped her goggles free of the water he splashed on her and braced herself. Her heart was beating a little faster than usual. She knew that it would be safe to go under the water, but she was still just a little scared.

"One," she said in a whisper and sank down in the water. "Two," she said, her chin dipping into the water. "Three!" she squeaked out and was just about to dunk her head when she saw something very strange zip across the surface of the water. She gasped and accidentally got a mouth full of water. As she coughed and sputtered, Mouse came back to the surface.

"Rebekah, are you okay?" he asked as he swam close to her. "Did you go under?"

Rebekah was still coughing when she pointed her finger across the water in the direction of what she had seen. "Sh-shark!" she managed to cry out.

Chapter 4

"Shark?" Mouse laughed and shook his head. "Rebekah, we're in a lake!" he pointed out.

"Shark!" Rebekah shouted louder this time as she had seen a triangular fin zipping in the direction of a group of other swimmers. "Everyone get out of the water! There's a shark! There's a shark!" she splashed and screamed as loud as she could, hoping that no one would get hurt.

The other people in the water didn't exactly hear what she was screaming about, but with all the splashing and fuss she was making they decided to hurry out of the water.

"Is it a lake monster?" one of the other kids from her class asked as they all gathered on the sand together. The lifeguard had climbed down from his lifeguard stand to see what all the screaming was about.

"What's wrong? Is someone hurt?" he asked, his floatation device grasped tightly in his hand.

"There is a shark in the water!" Rebekah said in a high pitched voice. "How can you let people swim in a lake with a shark?" she demanded, her eyes wide and full of anger.

The other people around her all began to look at her very strangely. Mouse hung his head and sighed. The lifeguard narrowed his eyes as he looked at Rebekah.

"Young lady there is nothing funny about raising a false alarm. You should only shout and scream if you are actually in trouble!" he shook his head and stomped back to his lifeguard stand.

"I think a shark is plenty of trouble!" Rebekah shouted after him.

"Rebekah," Mouse cringed. "There are no sharks in lakes! They live in the ocean!"

"Oh, so a lake monster you'll believe, but you won't believe what your own best friend saw with her own two eyes?" she crossed her arms and stuck out her tongue at Mouse. "Fine, believe what you want, but there is a shark in the water!"

She frowned as she watched the other swimmers getting back into the water. She knew that no one believed her. If she hadn't seen it for herself, she wouldn't believe it either. But she had seen it. There was no question in her mind that there was a shark in the lake.

"I can't let all those people get eaten," she grumbled. Then she saw Mouse trudging back into the water.

"Mouse! Don't!" she gasped and ran over to him. "Please, I don't want you to be a shark snack!"

"Rebekah there is no shark in the lake!" he said with frustration.

"Oh yes, then what is that?" Rebekah said and pointed across the lake to where she saw the triangle zipping across the surface once more.

"Uh," Mouse's eyes widened. His breath grew short. "Uh," he repeated, his mouth dropping open.

"Shark," Rebekah said calmly. "Is the word that you're looking for."

"Shark!" Mouse screamed out and pointed at the triangular fin. "Shark!" he screamed again. This time no one in the water listened. They just kept swimming. But one person did hear Mouse's panicked screams.

"That's it," the lifeguard said as he walked up behind them. "The two of you, get off of my beach!" he growled and pointed to the small fence that surrounded the shore line of the lake. "Now!"

"But there really is a shark-" Mouse said, pointing to the last place he saw it. The fin was gone and the lifeguard was still angry.

"If you two don't get off this beach right now I'll make sure you're banned for life!" he said with a huff. "There is nothing funny about faking an emergency!"

Mouse grabbed Lochness from his pool.

"Fine," Rebekah said with her chin lifted in the air. "Who would want to swim in a shark infested lake anyway?"

Chapter 5

As Rebekah and Mouse walked off the beach, Rebekah heard her friends and other swimmers splashing and laughing in the water.

"Mouse wait," she frowned as she looked back at the water. "We can't just leave them to be eaten."

"Rebekah you heard the lifeguard," Mouse warned her. "If he catches us on the beach again, we could get into real trouble."

"If we don't do anything then we'll be hearing about shark attacks on the news tonight," Rebekah pointed out. "We can't just pretend we didn't see the shark."

"Maybe it wasn't a shark," Mouse pointed out. "Maybe it was just a reflection of the sun on the water, or a piece of a tree branch floating."

Rebekah shook her head firmly. "I know what I saw and it was not a reflection or a tree branch. It was a shark!"

"It seems so impossible," Mouse sighed.

"This from the boy who believes in lake monsters?" Rebekah asked with a raised eyebrow.

"I didn't say I believe in them. I just said there was a lot of information about them," he corrected her.

"Well, even if it's not a shark, I think we need to figure out what it is, don't you?" she smiled a smile that Mouse knew all too well.

"Oh boy," he sighed.

"That's right Mouse, we have ourselves a mystery!" Rebekah said with a gleam in her eyes and a determined grimace. "Whatever is in that lake is going to wish it never messed with us!"

"But Rebekah, what if it really is a shark?" Mouse asked nervously as he trailed after her. "I don't think I want to be a shark snack."

"Don't worry," Rebekah smiled as they picked their way down a thin trail through some trees that led back down to the water. "We won't get too close. Trust me!"

"That's what you always say!" Mouse groaned and followed after her. Rebekah was well known for solving mysteries in her small town. However, sometimes she was also the one who made them. And Mouse was usually stuck right in the middle of the mystery!

Chapter 6

Rebekah peeked around the trees at the lifeguard stand. She could see him scanning the swimmers. He was doing his best to keep them safe. However if he saw Rebekah and Mouse getting back in the water he would be furious.

"Pst, come this way," Rebekah said when she spotted an old row boat that was pulled up on the sand.

"He'll spot us in that!" Mouse protested.

"Not if we're under it," Rebekah grinned. She flipped the boat over and floated it in the water. Then Mouse swam underneath. Rebekah lifted the edge so she wouldn't actually have to put her head under the water.

"Look it even has eyes," Rebekah grinned as she pointed to the two holes near the front of the boat. "I guess someone left it here because of these," she peeked through the holes. "Perfect, I can see everything that is happening on the lake. Now we just have to wait for the shark to show up again."

"What are we going to do if it does?" Mouse asked.

"I'm not sure, catch it maybe," Rebekah said with a shrug.

"How exactly are we going to catch a shark?" Mouse gasped.

"I'm not sure yet," Rebekah said with a frown. "But I'm sure I'll think of something!"

As she shuffled her feet through the sand on the bottom of the lake she felt something like rope under them.

"What's this?" she wondered and tugged at it with her toes. It lifted up from the sand but he could not pull it all the way up.

"Mouse, there's something down there," she said with surprise as she tugged at the rope harder.

"What is it?" Mouse asked as he tried to peer down through the water.

"I don't know, but we should see what it is," Rebekah said quickly.

"You mean, I should?" Mouse sighed as he knew that Rebekah would not swim under the water.

"Could you?" she smiled sweetly and clasped her hands together, pleading with him.

"Of course," Mouse said with a grin. He dove down into the water and swam to the bottom. When he brushed his fingers through the sand he felt the rope as well. He grabbed it and gave it a hard tug. When he did, an entire net came up from the sandy floor. He swam up to the surface with it.

"Look at this!" he said as he splashed up through the water. "It's an old net!"

"Perfect!" Rebekah clapped her hands. "We can use that to catch the shark!"

"Rebekah," Mouse said with a glare. "I will swim under water. I will hide from the lifeguard. I will even hide out under a row boat. But I will not try to catch a shark!"

Rebekah nodded as if she was listening, but she was already looking out through the holes in the row boat. She was searching for any sign of the shark on the water. So far all she saw were her friends splashing and swimming. Then she saw it. It was further out on the lake than it had been before. But she could still see it. The gray triangle fin was zipping back and forth across the water!

"Sh-shark!" Rebekah cried out. She began pushing the row boat forward in the water.

"Rebekah slow down!" Mouse pleaded as he tried to keep up with how fast she was pushing the row boat.

"No way," Rebekah shouted back. "I'm going shark fishing!"

Chapter 7

Rebekah kept the row boat moving forward with determination. She ignored the fact that the water was getting deeper and it would not be too long until she was walking on her tip toes. She just had to get to that shark.

"There he is," Rebekah hissed when she saw the fin zip past their row boat in the other direction. She sloshed the boat to the side and continued in the direction of the shark. Mouse was doing his best to keep up without losing his footing in the soft sand. All he could see was the back of Rebekah's head; he couldn't see the shark fin that she was seeing.

"We have to get a picture!" he said quickly. "If we get a picture then everyone will have to believe us!"

"A picture?" Rebekah shook her head. "Oh no way, we're getting ourselves a shark."

"Rebekah," Mouse argued. "We are never going to be able to catch a shark."

"Alright fine," Rebekah nodded. "If we can't catch the shark then we will just take a picture. Then at least that pesky lifeguard will have to believe us."

The lifeguard was watching the row boat drifting across the water. He had no idea where it came from, but he guessed it had gotten loose from someone's dock. As long as it didn't drift into the swimming area it was not really a danger, but he was keeping an eye on it, as it still seemed odd to him. While the children laughed and had a great time in the water, Rebekah and Mouse crept closer to the shark. They were almost on top of it, when it suddenly bolted the other way.

"Argh!" Rebekah growled. "This shark doesn't know which way he wants to go!" she jerked the row boat in the same direction the shark had gone in. Suddenly, she felt the sand disappearing beneath her feet.

"Oh no, I can't touch!" she gasped and started to panic.

"It's okay," Mouse assured her. "Just hold on to the sides of the boat," he showed her where to put her hands. "See? As long as it's floating, you won't sink. We can kick our feet to keep the boat moving."

"Thank you," Rebekah sighed, feeling a little better. But she was still nervous. As they drew closer and closer to the shark, the water was getting deeper and deeper. She was sure that she was further out in the lake now than she had ever been before.

"Maybe we should just get a picture," Rebekah said quietly. "I see the shark coming closer, hand me your camera," she reached for it. Mouse handed it to her. Mouse pushed the row boat up with his hands so that the edge of it tipped up enough that Rebekah could snap a picture. It was not easy to do as his feet were not touching either. The moment the lip of the row boat tipped up, Rebekah found herself face to fin!

"Ah!" Rebekah shrieked and the camera went off with a bright flash.

"Ah!" Mouse reeled backwards and the row boat dropped down on top of them with a splash.

"Go fast!" Rebekah gasped out as she grabbed on to the sides of the row boat. Mouse and Rebekah began kicking their feet so fast that they were churning up a lot of water.

"I don't think we're getting anywhere," Rebekah frowned and took a deep breath. 'We shouldn't be running anyway. We need to stop this shark from scaring everyone!"

"Rebekah, this is serious," Mouse warned. "We could be eaten!"

"We're not going to be eaten," Rebekah promised him. "We're going to stop this once and for all." She grabbed the old fishing net and looked Mouse in the eyes. "Ready?"

Mouse nodded slowly. "One, two, three," he said quickly and then held his nose as he dove down under the water. On three Rebekah closed her eyes tightly and braced herself as she ducked down under the water. She swam under the edge of the row boat and was on her way back up when she saw legs kicking in the water in front of her with huge flippers sticking out from them. When she reached the surface she was too shocked to realize what she had just done.

"Good job Rebekah!" Mouse said proudly.

Rebekah was staring at the shark fin that was floating across the water not far from them.

"Mouse," she said in a dazed voice. "Maybe there really are lake monsters."

"Why do you say that?" Mouse asked curiously.

"Because, that shark has feet!" Rebekah shook her head in amazement.

Chapter 8

"Feet?" Mouse gasped. "Sharks definitely don't have feet," he frowned. Rebekah was already gathering up the net that they had found.

"Oh no!" she hissed. "You're not getting away from me!" with that she swam after the fin as best as she could while carrying the net.

"Rebekah be careful!" Mouse pleaded and swam after her. The fin just continued to pull far enough away that Rebekah could not reach it. She decided to go under the water again. This time she didn't have to count. She ducked right under and peered through her goggles at the strange flippers. She saw the legs kicking casually in the water. Rebekah reached out and grabbed one of the creature's ankles. The creature began to kick and twist causing a lot of splashing on the surface. Rebekah let go and swam up through the water to gulp down some air. The creature was splashing and sloshing in the water in a bit of a panic. The lifeguard saw all of the splashing and churning of the water from his lifeguard stand.

"I'm coming!" he shouted, thinking that there was a swimmer in trouble. He raced across the beach and dove right into the water. He swam swiftly through the water until he reached Rebekah, Mouse, and the shark. When he surfaced from the water and saw Rebekah and Mouse he was very angry.

"What is this? Another hoax?" he demanded as he looked between the two of them. "Didn't I tell you to leave the beach?"

"But! We found the shark!" Rebekah protested.

"For the last time young lady there is no shark in this lake! This is a lake! Sharks live in the ocean!" he splashed his hand in the water as if to make his point. Right beside him the shark fin floated up in the water. "Ah!" he screamed when he saw it. "Shark!"

In one swift move he flipped the rowboat over and tossed Rebekah and Mouse inside of it. He was scrambling to climb in himself when the rest of the shark emerged from the water. First its head, then its shoulders, then the rest of his body.

Chapter 9

"What is that?" the lifeguard asked.

"I'm pretty sure it's not a shark," Rebekah said with a frown.

"Or a lake monster," Mouse admitted with a blush.

"But we did catch it," Rebekah pointed out. As she was speaking the creature stopped splashing. What they saw was a strange helmet, and goggles.

"You're no shark or lake monster at all!" she pointed a finger in the creature's direction. "Take that thing off and show us who you are."

"Okay, okay," a muffled voice said. Two hands rose up out of the water and tugged the helmet free of his head. The boy who stared at them looked about three or four years older than Rebekah and Mouse.

"Why in the world are you going around here as if you are a shark?" Rebekah demanded. As she asked the row boat they were in began to sink. It was clear that the holes she had been spying on the shark through were now causing the boat to fill with water.

"I wasn't acting like a shark," he said with a frown. "And what are you thinking pulling on someone's leg while they are under the water? You could have really hurt me!" he narrowed his eyes at Rebekah.

"Well when you pretend to be a lake monster and scare everyone that could really hurt someone too!" Mouse pointed out with a shake of his head. "It's not funny to get everyone so worked up."

"I have no idea what you're talking about!" the boy protested. "I was trying out my new diving suit!"

"Diving suit?" Rebekah asked, then she felt the water rising up over her feet in the boat. "Uh oh!" she gasped out.

"Everybody out!" the lifeguard cried out and tossed Rebekah and Mouse back into the water before jumping back in himself. "Look I don't know what kind of prank the three of you were pulling, but it is never a good idea to pretend to be in danger in the water," with that he started to swim off. Then he stopped and called back over his shoulder. "And always check your row boat for holes!"

"We will!" Mouse waved as the lifeguard swam away. "I hope he lets us back on the beach," he winced.

"He will," Rebekah said with confidence. "After all we did solve the shark mystery."

"Why do you keep talking about a shark?" the boy asked with a frown. "This is a lake, there are no sharks in a lake!"

"Well you sure looked like one," Rebekah pointed out with a frown. "In fact, I was sure you were a shark."

"Or a lake monster," Mouse piped up from beside Rebekah.

"I'm neither," the boy said. "My name is Tony, and I invented this diving suit."

"You invented it?" Rebekah said with surprise. "That must have taken a lot of work."

"It did," he said with a glare. "That's why I don't want people tugging on my legs under the water. You could have hurt some of the equipment."

"Sorry," Rebekah sighed. "I was just trying to keep everyone in the water safe."

"Well, I need to get back to work," Tony said. "I've been searching the bottom of the lake for trash and treasure."

"Oh that sounds like fun!" Rebekah smiled. "That's what I was going to do with my goggles."

"Well with my oxygen tanks I can stay under the water for a lot longer," Tony explained and turned around to show them the tanks strapped to his back. One of the flaps that connected the tanks to his diving suit had come loose, and was sticking straight up, just like a triangle!

"There's the fin!" Rebekah cried out and tugged on Mouse's arm. "Look!"

Mouse saw it too and had to laugh. "Wow you fooled us without even meaning to!"

Tony looked over his shoulder and saw the flap. "Oh that isn't good!" he gasped as he fastened the flap. "I usually check all of my equipment during a dive. It must have come loose somehow."

He shook his head as he turned back to look at them. "It's a good thing you two tried to catch me. It's not safe to go diving without all of my equipment set up properly. Thanks a lot!"

Rebekah smiled proudly and winked lightly at Mouse. "Well maybe we didn't catch a shark, but we still did save the day!"

"Hm, I still say there could be real lake monsters," Mouse pointed out.

"Well if there's one in this lake, I'll find it!" Tony said with a grin and pulled his helmet back on top of his head. Before pulling it down he smiled at Rebekah.

"If you really want to find some treasure, there's a great spot over there," he pointed toward the shore. "It's shallow enough that you can get a good look with just your goggles!" Then he pulled his helmet down on top of his head again. He gave them both a wave before diving back under the water. The last thing they saw were his large flippers wiggling underneath the surface.

"Wow that would be amazing to try!" Mouse said with a grin. "I bet I could even bring Lochness in that suit with me."

"I don't think so," Rebekah laughed. "What if he got loose?"

Mouse's eyes widened. "Good point," he shuddered.

"Let's go check out the spot he was talking about!" Rebekah suggested. They gave the row boat a solid tug and were able to get it to float toward the shore. Once they had the row boat back on land, they jumped back into the water. Rebekah pulled her goggles down over her eyes and ducked right under the water. She didn't even think about it! Under the water they found the treasure that Tony was talking about. There were tiny rocks in all different shapes and colors. There was also a lost shoe, a swimming turtle, and a silver coin. Rebekah brought up each item for Mouse to see. They collected their treasure in the row boat. Every time they went to the lake to swim, they would stop by the row boat to look at their treasure. Then they would search the lake for more! Soon other kids wanted to see the treasure too. The row boat became a museum at the lake.

"How in the world did this happen?" Rebekah's mother asked one day when she saw the row boat museum.

"Well," Rebekah sighed. "It all started with a shark in the lake!"

"A lake monster!" Mouse corrected her.

"Rebekah, there are no sharks in the lake, and there are no lake monsters," her mother said.

"Tell that to Tony!" Rebekah grinned and Mouse laughed.

Rebekah – Girl Detective #8

Magic
Gone Wrong!

PJ Ryan

Rebekah - Girl Detective #8
Magic Gone Wrong!

Chapter 1

Rebekah was walking along the sidewalk toward the park. Mouse was supposed to meet her, so that they could spend the afternoon searching for acorns. Then they could use the acorns to lure out squirrels. Rebekah had a theory that the squirrels had a secret treasure trove of all kinds of items that had gone missing around town, not just acorns. She hoped that if the squirrels took the acorns, then they would lead Rebekah straight to the missing items. As she was thinking about this, she heard the pounding of footsteps behind her.

"You will not believe what I saw last night!" Mouse cried out as he ran up to Rebekah. She turned around quickly with a smile.

"What?" Rebekah asked eagerly. She was always curious. In fact she was known around her small town for being a great detective. At least, she liked to think so. There wasn't a mystery that Rebekah left unsolved.

"Magic!" he declared and waved his hands above his head as if he was sprinkling glitter. "The most amazing, phenomenal, fantastic show on Earth!"

"Magic?" Rebekah replied with a sigh and pressed her fingertips to her forehead. "Have you been watching cartoons again Mouse? I've told you this before, you're really much too old for cartoons," she said sternly.

"No," Mouse said and blushed. He did like his cartoons, but he wasn't going to tell Rebekah that. "I watched the famous Feary Disappeary!"

"Feary Disappeary?" Rebekah furrowed a brow as she tried to remember if she knew that name from anywhere. "Is that a real name?"

"Well, it's probably his stage name," Mouse admitted with a shrug. "But his tricks were amazing!"

"Did you hear that word?" Rebekah asked as she stopped and looked straight at her friend.

"What word?" he asked with a frown.

"Tricks," she replied. "Everyone knows that magic is all a bunch of tricks, there is nothing real about it. Clever, yes, but real, no! Now hurry, we have to catch some thieving squirrels."

"Okay that's true of some tricks," Mouse admitted. "But you can't say that about all magic. There are some tricks no one can figure out!"

"I can figure out any magic trick," Rebekah said firmly as they walked into the park.

"Is that so?" Mouse asked and pushed his glasses up on his nose. "Then maybe you should watch the show with me and tell me how he does all of his tricks."

"Will it be on again?" Rebekah asked, ready to take the challenge.

"No," Mouse frowned. "It was one night only. But I know what we can do!" he snapped his fingers and then turned around on the sidewalk. "We can go on his website, and you can see all of the tricks for yourself."

Rebekah glanced at her watch. She didn't really want to miss the squirrels. When Mouse looked back at her pleadingly, she could see how important it was to him.

"Alright," she sighed and followed him back to his house. They sat in front of the computer together while Mouse typed in the site for the magician. It was full of flashy designs and video clips of the magician's tricks.

"Here look at this one," Mouse smiled and clicked on one of the videos. When it had barely begun to play Rebekah rolled her eyes.

"Oh I know how to do that," she said as the magician showed how he could link two metal rings together.

"Really?" Mouse asked skeptically.

"Yes, one of the rings has a small break in it, allowing the rings to snag together," Rebekah said confidently.

"Oh," Mouse frowned. "I guess that could be right."

"How about this one?" he asked and clicked on another video.

"Oh I don't have to watch the show," Rebekah shrugged. "Just tell me the tricks that had you baffled, and I'll show you how your magician did the job."

"No way," Mouse said with surprise. "You couldn't really do it," he shook his head.

"Try me," Rebekah smirked. She was certain that she could.

Chapter 2

They left Mouse's house and began walking to the park again as Mouse thought about what tricks might stump Rebekah. He was still thinking about it when they reached the park. The park was busy with kids they knew from the neighborhood and from school. The sun was bright in the sky. There were plenty of birds flying from branch to branch. There were also plenty of squirrels who looked pretty crafty. Rebekah looked the little thieves in the eyes, as if warning them that she had not forgotten about their sticky fingers. They walked over to a shady area where there was a picnic bench and green grass around it.

"Okay," Mouse sat down on the wooden bench and thought a moment. "Well there was this trick where he turned water into lava! That was pretty fantastic!" He remembered how the audience had gasped and cheered when the water shifted colors.

"Lava?" Rebekah said skeptically. "You mean he turned clear water into red water?" she grinned, as she was sure she had figured it out.

"Well, yes but he called it lava," Mouse frowned. "I mean it was much more magical on the screen, with all the smoke and flashing lights."

"I bet," Rebekah grinned as she sat down beside him. "Okay what else?" Rebekah asked.

"I'm not sure," Mouse rubbed his chin slowly. "Oh yes! He turned a rabbit into a bird!" he said and shook his head. "It was amazing. This cute fluffy little bunny became this huge winged bird. The bird flew away and everything!"

"Okay," Rebekah said, her smirk turning into a smile. "Anything else?"

"Well the most amazing trick was the disappearing act!" Mouse sighed as he shook his head. "I just don't know how he could make his assistant disappear!"

"Hm," Rebekah grinned and wiggled her toes under the picnic table. "I think I do."

"How?" Mouse asked, amazed and eager to hear how the trick was done. "Tell me!"

Rebekah stood up from the picnic bench. "I can do way better than that," she said. "I'll show you! Stay here, because when I get back, you're going to be my assistant!"

As she ran off down the street Mouse stared after her. He knew that Rebekah was very smart, but he was sure she was no magician.

Chapter 3

Rebekah hurried back home to collect a few things. First she mixed together a pitcher of lemonade. Then she grabbed a clear cup from the shelf. She tossed this in her bag. She also took a small packet from the cabinet and tucked it into her bag. She grabbed some markers, scissors, and some string just in case. She smiled at herself in the mirror as she passed by it in the hall. Today she was not going to be a detective. Today she was going to be a magician! On the way back to the park she stopped by Mr. Douglas' appliance store. He always let her check out the merchandise when he got a new fancy appliance. He got a kick out of the idea that Rebekah liked to discover all there was to know about appliances. Rebekah thought they were pretty interesting, considering they could do so much. She had once spent a week documenting and inspecting the toaster in their kitchen. When her father finally asked her why, she announced that the toaster might just change the world one day if it was allowed to live up to its potential.

"Hi Rebekah!" Mr. Douglas said cheerfully. "Have you come in for a look at the new washer?"

"Not today," Rebekah shook her head. "Though I'm sure it's great."

"Well then how can I help you?" he asked with a smile.

"I need the biggest box you have!" Rebekah announced.

"Hm, well," he rapped his knuckles lightly on the counter. "Then I have just the place for you," he led her around the corner of the store and out behind it, near the dumpsters.

"The dumpsters?" Rebekah asked and pinched her nose to keep the smell out.

"No, over here," Mr. Douglas said and pointed to a huge pile of boxes. There were boxes of every shape, color and size. "Take any box you like," he said with a wave. "I have to get back to my customers!"

Rebekah picked out the biggest box she could find. It once held a refrigerator inside. She smiled.

"This will be perfect!"

Juggling the box, the bag, and the pitcher of lemonade, she started down the sidewalk back toward the park. In her mind she was already planning all of the tricks that she would show Mouse to prove that there was no such thing as real magic. Along the way she called out to anyone she saw on the street.

"Magic show at the park! Don't miss it!" she knew that an audience was very important for any type of show. When she made it back to the park, she peeked over the top of the box, looking for Mouse.

"Help!" she gurgled out as she almost dropped the pitcher of lemonade in her hand.

"What do you have all that for?" Mouse laughed as he hurried over to help her. The kids that were playing on the playground were curious too. When they saw Rebekah's red hair, they knew just who it was behind that large box. They all came running to see what kind of mystery Rebekah was about to unravel.

"What are you up to Rebekah?" one of the kids asked as they all did their best to help unload Rebekah.

"I'm going to put on a magic show!" Rebekah said with a smile as she thanked each of them for their help. "It's free for everyone, so please be here to watch!"

"I love magic!" one of the kids she knew from the neighborhood said.

"Me too," Mouse grinned as he looked over the assortment of items that Rebekah had brought back with her.

"Well this isn't your typical magic show," Rebekah warned. "There won't be any special lighting or wild music, only truth. I'm going to prove once and for all that there is no such thing as real magic," Rebekah said sternly. "Just give me a few minutes to set up, and then I will put on the show for all of you."

Chapter 4

"Let's give her some space," Mouse said and led the other kids over to the playground. He was feeling pretty confident that magic was one thing Rebekah would not be able to pull off. "Look who I brought with me today," Mouse showed his friends the pet he had brought along with him to the park. It was a little white mouse. Mouse got his nickname because he always had a mouse of some kind with him wherever he went.

"This is little Houdini," he said. He placed the mouse down in the grass and showed them how fast the mouse could run. All of the kids took a turn racing Houdini from one end of the sandbox to the other. Houdini always won!

"Alright everyone!" Rebekah called out across the park. "The show is ready!"

Once all the kids were sitting down in front of the grassy area where Rebekah had set up her show, she waved her magic wand high in the air. It was made of a stick she had found with a shiny stone tied to the top.

"I am here to show you all that any magic trick, is just that, a trick!" she said with a grin. "But first I will need a lovely assistant."

Some of the kids in the audience raised their hands, but Rebekah pointed at Mouse. "You there, Mouse, will you be my lovely assistant?"

"Well I don't know about lovely," Mouse chuckled and blushed as he stepped up beside Rebekah.

"For my first trick, I will turn an ordinary cup of lemonade into a cup of grape juice!" she declared happily and placed a clear cup on the picnic table nearby. Next she picked up the pitcher of lemonade she had brought from home. She poured lemonade into the cup.

233

"Now Mouse take a sip, so that everyone can be sure that it is actually lemonade," she instructed calmly.

Mouse picked up the clear cup and took a small sip. His lips puckered and his eyes squinted.

"Oh yeah, that's lemonade, and it could use a bit more sugar."

Rebekah stuck out her tongue as she had made the lemonade herself. "Now watch closely everyone as I transform this lemonade into grape juice!"

She waved her hand and wand over the cup. Then she tapped the edge of the cup twice with the tip of her wand. No one saw the purple powder that drifted from the end of the wand and into the lemonade. But they all saw the purple color start to appear in the lemonade, growing and growing, until the lemonade turned all the way purple, just like grape juice!

The kids all cheered in amazement that she had been able to transform the lemonade to grape juice with just the tap of her wand.

"Okay," she said and tossed the grape juice aside before anyone could figure out that it still tasted like lemonade.

Chapter 5

"For my next trick, I will turn a rabbit, into a mouse!"

She held up a stuffed rabbit that she had brought from her house. "A perfectly ordinary stuffed rabbit," she said and waved her wand right over the top of its head. "Nothing mousey about it!" She dropped the stuffed rabbit into a cardboard box on the picnic table. Then she reached into her pocket and pulled out a large handkerchief, all balled up. She accidentally dropped the handkerchief into the box and then spread it out over the top of the box.

"Alright for this trick to work, I need everybody to be clapping their hands," Rebekah insisted. All of the kids began to clap their hands loudly.

"Good, louder!" Rebekah called out as she tapped lightly at the handkerchief. "Ooga, booga, bunny be gone!" she announced, and then whipped the handkerchief off of the top of the box. All of the kids gasped and stopped clapping as they waited to see if the trick had worked. Rebekah scooped the mouse up out of the box, and held it out for everyone to see.

"Houdini!" Mouse cried out with surprise. He reached into his pocket, searching for his mouse friend. But he wasn't there. Somehow Rebekah had made him appear! Since everyone was so busy trying to figure out just how the mouse had appeared, no one noticed that the stuffed rabbit was still in the box, hidden under the handkerchief. The kids in the audience all clapped and cheered. When Rebekah tried to hand Houdini over to Mouse, the little escape artist managed to leap to the grass below. He scampered beneath the picnic table.

"Oh look, I made the mouse disappear too!" Rebekah laughed.

"Houdini!" Mouse cried out. All of the kids watching the show laughed. They laughed harder when Mouse dove under the table to try to catch Houdini. He nearly knocked over the table as he squirmed underneath it. Houdini bolted out on the other side and across the grass.

"Wait, come back!" Mouse called out.

"Is he hopping, like a rabbit?" one of the kids giggled.

"Doesn't look like it," another kid answered. "But Mouse sure is!"

Mouse was hopping over picnic tables and tree stumps as he chased after the mouse. When he finally managed to get a hold of the mouse he sighed and shook his head. He jogged back over to the picnic table with Houdini safely tucked back into his pocket.

"That one always gets away," Rebekah laughed as Mouse tried to catch his breath.

Chapter 6

"Alright Mouse, you're next," Rebekah said with a sneaky grin.

"Next for what?" Mouse asked innocently. So far all of Rebekah's tricks had worked out fairly well, but he knew that she had something big planned for the final trick.

"Next to disappear!" she announced with a wild wave of her wand.

"No way!" one of the kids in the audience cried out. "You can't make him disappear!" All of the kids were certain that this was one trick that Rebekah would not be able to pull off. Rebekah didn't mind. She knew exactly what she was doing. She walked over to the large cardboard box which she had spent a lot of time preparing.

"Just an ordinary box," she announced to her audience. "There is no hidden portal to another universe or time," she said as she pulled back the curtain that covered the front of the large cardboard box. "See? Nothing inside!" she announced. She cleared her throat and stood up on her tip toes.

"Now, for our final act," she said in a dramatic voice. "I will make this young man disappear!"

Mouse gulped and looked out at the audience of his friends and neighbors. He waved to them as if it might be the last chance he would have to wave.

"Please be careful Rebekah," he whispered nervously as he stepped into the box. Rebekah rolled her eyes, as she knew he wouldn't actually disappear. She dropped the curtain down in front of him.

"Now make sure you stay all the way to the back," she said in her dramatic voice. "Otherwise the magic might transport you to the wrong place!" she tried not to giggle.

She swung her wand high in the air making swirls and loops as if she was writing in the air. Then she walked all around the box, giving it a hard tap on each side she passed. "To make someone disappear takes all of the skill and strength of magic," she announced with a small grin. "Or does it?"

When she returned to the front, she tapped the side of the box sharply three times with her wand.

"One, two, three," she said to the audience with a grin. "And Mouse is history!" she swung the curtain back to reveal that the box was empty inside! The kids in the audience all cheered. Some whispered about how it was possible, and where Mouse might have gone.

"Yes the great Rebekah has caused Mouse to completely disappear. Where has he gone? How can the laws of physics be so easily defied?" she flipped her red curls over her shoulder and grinned. "Most importantly, when will he come back?" Rebekah said quickly, her eyes shining with amusement. "It will not take me long to bring him back!"

Rebekah waved her magic wand again, she swirled it through the air and swung it up and down. Then she pushed the wand through a slot in the side of the box. She felt the flap of cardboard that she had loosened when she tapped on the side of the box, fold back up.

Rebekah had created the illusion of Mouse disappearing by using an extra piece of cardboard. When he stepped into the box it was folded up against the side. Rebekah had him stand in the back of the box. When she tapped on the side of the box, the cardboard unfolded.

When she opened the curtain, it looked like the extra piece of cardboard was actually the back of the box. Of course Rebekah would be the only one who knew that Mouse had been behind the partition the entire time.

Now it was time for the big reveal, and she was very excited. Barely able to hide her giggling she waved her wand a final time.

Chapter 7

"Bippity, boppity, Mouse!" she declared and whipped back the curtain from the front of the box. The cardboard flap had folded back as she planned, but only to reveal the actual back of the box. Mouse was still nowhere to be seen.

"This is impossible," Rebekah said quietly to herself as she studied the box.

"Mouse?" she called out and poked her head inside the box. She wondered if she might have somehow done the trick wrong. "Hello?" she called out again. The audience was getting a little restless.

"Where is he?" they all began asking. Some even began chanting very loudly.

"Bring Mouse back, bring Mouse back, bring Mouse back!" They clapped their hands and stomped their feet at the same time.

Rebekah stepped all the way inside of the cardboard box. She tested the sides of it by pushing lightly on them with her hands. She walked to the back of the box, and then back to the front. She pushed her feet against the grass to make sure there wasn't a hole hidden somewhere. Finally she stepped back out of the box. She stood outside of the box for a long moment and stared at it with narrowed eyes.

"But he can't actually be gone," Rebekah murmured to herself. She tipped the box backward to be sure that she was not somehow overlooking Mouse. But there was simply no one inside, it was completely empty. "Where did he go?" Rebekah frowned as she glanced under the picnic table.

"You lost him?" one of the kids shouted out and stood up from the grass. "What kind of magician loses their lovely assistant?"

"Obviously he's not lost," Rebekah snapped back, feeling a little frightened. "He couldn't really disappear. Magic isn't real!" The kids who had been watching the show did not look so certain. In fact some of them looked a little angry.

"Then where is he?" another of the kids questioned. "Why can't you bring him back?"

"He's not missing," Rebekah said firmly. "He's just misplaced," she reached up and tapped her chin lightly. "If I were Mouse, where would I be?" she muttered to herself.

As she walked across the grass the entire crowd of kids stood up as well. They walked after her, curious to see what she would do, and whether this might all be part of the show. They were all a little worried too, that Mouse might really be missing. Rebekah checked on the playground. But Mouse was not on the swings, or the merry go round, or even on the slide. She checked near the water, but again, Mouse was nowhere to be seen.

"You!" she pointed at one of the boys in the audience. "Check in the bathroom!"

The young boy did as he was told. When he came back out of the bathroom he shook his head sadly.

"Rebekah I think you really made him disappear," he frowned. "Will he ever come back?"

"Impossible!" Rebekah cried out as she looked down at her homemade wand. "Magic isn't real," she said more to herself this time, than to the other kids. With her head hung in thought she walked back toward the area where she had set up her magic show.

"Maybe if I try again," she said as she walked up to the cardboard box. She closed the curtain. She walked around the box, tapping each side. Then she stopped at the front of the box and tapped her wand on the curtain.

"Bippity, boppity, Mouse!" she said loudly and whacked the curtain hard. All of the kids were quiet as they waited to see if her plan had worked. Rebekah whipped back the curtain, hoping to reveal that Mouse had returned. However, once again, the box was completely empty.

"Mouse!" Rebekah sniffled as her panic shifted to feeling very guilty. "Where are you?" she didn't care if the other kids doubted her now. She just wanted her best friend back. "Oh what have I done?" she cried out to the sky, waving her hands in the air. "I should never have said magic wasn't real! Now magic has had its revenge!"

The other kids all looked at each other strangely. They had never seen Rebekah act quite this oddly before.

"It's okay Rebekah," one of her friends from school said gently. "I'm sure he'll come back one day."

"Who's going to tell his parents?" one of the other kids asked.

"Oh no!" Rebekah moaned and shook her head back and forth. "Why didn't I just believe him? Why did I have to prove that magic wasn't real?"

Rebekah fell to her knees in the grass and sunk her hands in her bright red hair. "Please! Come back Mouse! Come back!"

Chapter 8

Suddenly everyone heard a giggle from high above them.

"Mouse?" Rebekah looked up at the sky. "Is that you?" she asked hopefully.

"It is!" Mouse replied with a laugh.

"Oh no! I've not only made you disappear, now you're invisible! Why did I have to be such a good magician?!"

Mouse laughed harder. "Hello!" Mouse waved from a thick tree limb high above the magic show. He whipped a black cape over his shoulders and jumped down from the tree limb. He landed right in front of Rebekah and the other kids.

"Tada!" he said proudly.

"Mouse!" Rebekah growled and glared at him. "Were you up on that tree limb the whole time?"

"Of course I was," Mouse replied, and then giggled. "You didn't really think that I had disappeared, did you?"

All of the other kids laughed and cheered. "Mouse is the real magician!" one of the kids shouted out. Mouse took a deep bow and all of the kids clapped very loudly. All of the kids, except for Rebekah. In fact, she turned around and stomped off across the park.

"Uh oh," Mouse frowned.

"I don't think she's happy with you," one of the other kids said.

"Me either," Mouse scratched the top of his head. He started after Rebekah. "Rebekah! Wait!" he called after her. Rebekah just continued to stomp off across the grass. Her cheeks were as red as her hair and her hands were balled into fists.

"Rebekah please!" Mouse sighed. "I didn't mean to make you so mad."

"I'm not mad!" Rebekah shouted, and then cleared her throat. "Okay maybe I'm a little mad," she mumbled.

"Well why are you mad?" Mouse asked with a lopsided grin. "Is it because magic just might be real?"

"It's not real," Rebekah crossed her arms. "You just tricked me!"

Mouse grinned. "Okay yes I did trick you."

"But how?" Rebekah asked. "How in the world did you get out of that box?"

"A good magician never tells his secrets!" Mouse insisted. "Now come on back and we can do a few more tricks."

Chapter 9

Rebekah planted her feet firmly in the green grass and narrowed her eyes sharply. "Mouse, I am not going anywhere until you tell me exactly how you did that trick!"

"Oh fine," Mouse laughed again. "How about if I show you instead?"

"Sounds great," Rebekah nodded and they walked together back to the picnic table where the magic show had taken place. All of the other kids had gone back to the playground.

"Look, I knew that you wanted to prove to me that magic isn't real," Mouse said calmly as he walked over to the cardboard box. "I know that most of the magic tricks I see aren't real," he explained. "But it is still fun to enjoy the show, and wonder, if it might be possible. You know to me, the only thing that is impossible is knowing everything."

Rebekah tilted her head from side to side. "I guess you're right about that," she nodded slowly. "It would be pretty hard to know everything."

"So while you were teaching me a lesson, I decided to teach you one," Mouse said trying to hide a smile.

"Oh you sneaky little Mouse!" Rebekah huffed and crossed her arms. "You planned this didn't you?"

"Maybe," he winked lightly at her. "You see, after you put me inside of the box, before you walked around it, I had one of the other kids from the audience cut a little slit in the back of the box. Just big enough for me to be able to squeeze through. I knew it would be hard for you to notice it."

He paused behind the box and showed her the cut from the bottom of the box to nearly the top. "Then I slipped out of the back of the box. I climbed the tree, and watched."

Rebekah was still pretty miffed that he would play such a trick on her. "Well it was very clever of you, but also very mean!" she frowned.

"I didn't mean to be mean," he promised as she walked back to the front of the box. "I just wanted you to see what it was like to not be able to solve a mystery for once!"

"I would have solved it," Rebekah said sternly. "I would have sooner or later!"

"I have a feeling I would have been up on that tree limb for a long time," Mouse laughed.

As they walked home Rebekah was fairly quiet.

"What's wrong?" Mouse asked. "You're not still mad at me are you?"

"No," she shook her head. "I was just thinking about whether Feary Disappeary does live shows."

"Sure he does, there's one next month!" Mouse said with a grin.

"Well I think we should go," Rebekah smiled widely. "I want another shot at figuring out all of his tricks!"

Mouse laughed and shook his head. "Always the detective!"

Next Steps

This book is part of the children's series, "Rebekah - Girl Detective".

I'd really love to hear from you!

I very much appreciate your reviews and comments so thank you in advance for taking a moment to leave one for "Rebekah - Girl Detective: Books 1-8".

You can join Rebekah's fun Facebook page for young detectives here:

http://www.facebook.com/RebekahGirlDetective

Sincerely,
PJ

All Titles by PJ Ryan Can be Found Here (Author Page)

http://www.amazon.com/author/pjryan

Look for the following series with more coming soon!

Rebekah – Girl Detective

RJ – Boy Detective

Mouse's Secret Club

Made in the USA
San Bernardino, CA
03 November 2019